NOT *MYSELF* TODAY

MURIEL ELLIS PRITCHETT

Black Rose Writing | Texas

Second Printing

ISBN: 978-1-68433-547-3
Library of Congress Control Number: 2020909601
PUBLISHED BY BLACK ROSE WRITING
www.blackrosewriting.com

Printed in the United States of America
Suggested Retail Price (SRP) $18.95

Not Myself Today is printed in Garamond

*As a planet-friendly publisher, Black Rose Writing does its best to
eliminate unnecessary waste to reduce paper usage and energy
costs, while never compromising the reading experience. As a result,
the final word count vs. page count may not meet common
expectations.

Not Myself Today is dedicated to my beautiful, talented, creative daughters, Heather Pritchett Hoogeveen and Heidi Pritchett Molley, who have patiently waited many years for this book to be published.

Special thanks to my publisher, *Black Rose Writing*, for kindly allowing me to step outside of my women's fiction genre to write a YA paranormal; to my "eagle eye" editor and cheerleader, Judy Purdy; to my Thursday Writers, who carefully critiqued this manuscript chapter by chapter; and to my computer guru husband, Harold Pritchett, who keeps my computer running and knows how to cook delicious takeout dinners from local restaurants when necessary.

NOT MYSELF TODAY

CHAPTER ONE
BEGINNING OF THE END

At first there was just darkness and nothingness. Then awareness began to creep in. Vague noises in the distance. Needle prickliness in my arms and legs. Explosive pain in my head. Waves of nausea. I moaned and squirmed in protest. Through swollen eyes, I squinted at blurry shapes. Trying to make some sense of what I was seeing and feeling, I reached out with my right hand and grabbed something solid. Cold, hard plastic. A bed rail? As my eyes slowly focused, I flinched at the sight of my trembling hand and gulped. *This hand wasn't mine!*

A cold sweat broke out across my upper lip. A chill ran down my back. My heart began to race. I looked at the white-knuckled hand, again. *Holy crap!* The fingernails were chewed down to the quick. My hand would have had a French manicure. *Hadn't I given up my daily fix of Cherry Cokes to pay for it?*

Pulling my left arm out from beneath the sheet, I saw it was encased in a black elastic wrist splint. I shuddered at the sight of a floral tattoo encircling the base of the middle finger. *No way!*

Dad would kill me if I ever got a tattoo. Only bikers, bad girls, and boozers had tattoos. A taste of acid burned in the back of my throat. *This hand wasn't mine either!*

Something was seriously wrong. *Seriously.*

This was the scariest, most real nightmare I'd ever had. But what if it wasn't a nightmare or a dream? What if all of this was real? I looked around the room and took a deep breath. It definitely looked and smelled like a hospital room. But if I really was in a hospital, why was I here? What had happened to me?

A strangled sound involuntarily escaped from my throat. As I closed my eyes tightly and gritted my teeth, fragments of memory flashed through my brain. My head pounded. I remembered running and kicking the ball down the soccer field with Rachel racing alongside. I kicked the ball past the goalkeeper and into the net. I heard the crowd roaring in my ears and felt the ground vibrating beneath my feet. I saw my teammates running and jumping and screaming, carrying me on their shoulders in victory, and then—nothing. *Absolutely nothing.* I, Lindsey Anderson, had kicked the winning goal for the state soccer championship, and now I couldn't remember anything else.

I opened my eyes, breathing hard, my heart racing. *Holy crap!* Something must have happened on the soccer field. Something so awfully bad that it landed me in the hospital. Yes! That had to be it! I must be unconscious or in a coma. Even now, in the real world—not this alternate reality—Dad would be sitting by my side, squeezing my hand, whispering in my ear how much he loved me. And Rachel? She would have to be in the corner bawling, worried sick that her BFF was going to die.

I let out the breath I had been holding. Yes, it all made perfect sense now. This room was a holding station—halfway between life and death. I closed my eyes, willing myself to wake up. *Nothing.* I gritted my teeth tighter and clinched my jaw, listening for sounds from the other side. Sounds from the real world. *"Wake up, Lindsey!"* I pleaded out loud, surprised by the sound of my hoarse voice, which sounded higher in pitch—a soprano voice like Rachel's. Not the alto voice I sang in choir.

But no matter how hard I tried, no matter how hard I strained to hear my daddy's voice or feel his hand on mine, nothing happened. No bright light at the end of a tunnel either. No angels singing in the heavens. No hands of dead relatives reaching out for me. *Nada. Zip. Zero. Absolutely nothing.*

So now what? Scared and trying to focus, I glanced around my "holding station" cubicle and noticed a small nightstand with an old beige phone, one of those bed-tray thingies on wheels, and a small sink with mirror. *Mirror?* I tried to sit up, but another wave of nausea swept over me. Why did my entire body hurt so much? I felt the panic rising in me, like a tsunami after an earthquake. *Stay calm, Lindsey. You can figure this out.*

Woozy, but determined, I slung my legs over the edge of the mattress and sat up. The faded blue gown I was wearing separated in the back, allowing a draft of cold air to ride up my spine. I shivered. *Could a head injury cause weird hallucinations?* Suddenly my teeth began to chatter uncontrollably, and I was having trouble getting my breath. I whimpered like a scared, little kid.

When I tried to stand up, a pain ripped through my side. I lifted up my gown and saw a wide bandage taped tightly across my ribs. *Did I injure myself during the game? Was I waking up from a 10-year coma?* That would explain why I didn't recognize my own hands.

But if I wasn't dead, if this really was a hospital room and not an alternate reality or purgatory, where was everyone? Why wasn't Dad here holding my hand? Why wasn't Rachel sitting nearby weeping for her BFF? Didn't anyone care about me? A lump formed in my throat. I wanted my dad.

Fighting for control, I struggled to my feet. Hunched over like an old woman, inch by painful inch, I dragged myself and the IV tree over to the sink and mirror. I gripped the counter edge and stared into the mirror at red-rimmed hazel eyes that gazed back at me from a bruised, swollen, gaunt face. A small bandage covered part of my forehead. The hair on the back of my neck stood up. A cry escaped from my throat. *Holy crap! That girl in the mirror wasn't me!*

Hands that didn't look like mine grabbed a fistful of straight, dirty-blonde hair, caked with dried blood. What I considered my most attractive feature—my short auburn curly hair—was gone. Also missing, the blue eyes I had inherited from my dad. I wailed aloud.

That hideous, gray-faced girl in the mirror looked half-dead. Had she been in an accident? Had someone beat her up? She was NOT me. *She was NOT Lindsey Anderson, Senior Female Athlete of the Year.* I gagged and dry-heaved into the sink before the room went black.

CHAPTER TWO
TWO DAYS BEFORE
THE BEGINNING OF THE END

Yikes! I was late! I yanked open the door to the back entrance of East Lake High and nearly collided with my BFF Rachel Adams.

"Happy birthday, Lindsey!" She handed me a small white box. "How does it feel to be 18?"

Grinning, I dropped my book bag to the floor and winced at a nagging little ache in my left shoulder. "Still not old enough to drink, so it's just another birthday." I grinned at her and pulled back the box lid. Inside was a Mama Rosa's Decadent Chocolate cupcake, piled high with swirls of fudgy chocolate frosting. "Chocolate! Yum!" I gave her a hug. Maybe the antioxidants in the chocolate would make me feel better.

"Your favorite cupcake," she gushed, pulling a Cherry Coke out of her bookbag. "And your very favorite drink."

Rachel, my best friend since kindergarten, knew me better than anyone else.

I stuffed the Cherry Coke into my book bag, but held onto my cupcake to eat after homeroom. Slipping the book bag over my shoulder, I grunted as the dull ache sharpened into a throb. Maybe I had pulled a muscle or something.

Rachel touched my arm. "Hey, you okay?"

I nodded. "Yeah, too many books, I guess."

"You got that right," Rachel agreed. "They should be digitalized on tablets."

I nodded and looked at the wall clock. "Holy crap! Less than five minutes until the bell." Late for homeroom one more time and I'd get written up.

"Better hurry." Rachel shouted over her shoulder as she walked rapidly away from me. "You will be oh so dead if you're late, again."

Didn't I know that? My homeroom teacher, Mrs. Petty, was strict. She prided herself on having no favorites—especially any popular jocks who felt entitled. Taking long strides, like the soccer player I was, I headed for my locker, reaching it in record time. I grabbed my combination lock and smiled at Taylor Jackson, starting pitcher for our baseball team. He slammed his locker door shut and gave me a wink that made my heart flutter.

"Good morning, Taylor." I smiled and felt my heart beat a little faster. We'd been flirting with each other since Rachel's New Year's Eve party.

Taylor stepped closer to my locker, smiled, and nodded.

I felt a bit of warmth on my cheeks. Maybe today would be the day that Taylor would ask me out.

"Lindsey, did I hear today's your birthday?"

I nodded. My mouth was too dry to swallow, and I couldn't form any words anyway. *Lindsey, stop it. You're acting like a little girl crushing on a star jock.* I pulled out my lock and yanked open the door. Immediately, I was slammed by a locker full of empty Cherry Coke cans loudly cascading to the floor. A "Happy Birthday" helium balloon popped out and floated to the ceiling. "Holy crap!" I yelled, as the empty cans clattered and rolled all over the hall floor.

Then seemingly out of nowhere, a "flash mob" of students appeared and started singing "Happy Birthday."

Taylor Jackson grinned and winked. "Better hurry. You don't want to be late to homeroom."

"Hey, people! The bell is fixing to ring. Get moving."

At the sound of Mr. Henson's deep bass voice, everyone disappeared, leaving me alone to face the assistant principal, a.k.a. Hatchet Man. No one wanted to have a run-in with him or you'd end up in detention until graduation. I slammed my locker door shut and started to run in the direction of homeroom, only to find my way blocked.

"Where do you think you're going, Miss Soccer Star?" he asked.

With my cupcake in one hand and my backpack strap in the other, I gave him my sweet and innocent look. "Homeroom? I can't be late, again."

He leaned into my face. "Not my problem." He pointed to the cans on the floor in front of my locker. "This your stuff?"

"Huh? Most definitely not!"

He wagged a finger in front of my face. "Did it come out of your locker?"

I gulped. "Yes, sir."

"Then it's yours, Anderson." Mr. Henson turned to Mr. Feeney, our janitor, who was holding a trash bag. Grabbing it from Mr. Feeney, he handed it to me. "You own it—you clean it up!"

"But . . ." Out of the corner of my eye, I caught a glimpse of Rachel desperately pointing at the clock and motioning to me. I waved my hands at the mess in the floor and rolled my eyes. I knew my friends who planned this birthday/locker surprise meant well, but holy crap, what a mess!

"Now!" Mr. Henson's voice thundered in my ears.

I dropped my backpack, kicking it up against the wall, sat my cupcake box next to it, and started stuffing cans in the bag. Rachel blew me a kiss and left. I yanked two more cans off the floor and hoped that this wasn't an omen as to how my birthday would turn out.

It was a very long day. By the time I made it home from soccer practice, I was totally wiped out. The big state championship game was tomorrow, and the coach wanted us to be ready. He expected me, Rachel, and the other two seniors on the team to help bring home the trophy. But my butt was dragging, my head hurt, and my jaw, neck, and shoulder ached. I hoped I wasn't coming down with something that would keep me from playing. I would have to get a good night's sleep and recharge before the game.

Dad all but leaped from his comfy leather recliner when I unlocked the front door. He rushed over and hugged me. "How's my birthday girl?" I relaxed into his arms. "To celebrate your special day, why don't you, Rachel, and I go to your favorite place for dinner—Ray's on the River? What do you say?"

I collapsed on the sofa. "Sounds good, Dad, but I don't know. I haven't had a really great day, and I'm feeling poopy."

Dad sat down next to me. "I have some news that may cheer you up."

My shoulders sagged. There was nothing he could say that would put a smile on my face right now. "What?"

"Coach Garfield called."

Now he had my attention. Last week I had tried out for the U.S. Youth Soccer Olympic Development Program. Coach Garfield was one of the coaches I'd met. "Dad! What did he say?"

Dad grinned like the Cheshire Cat in *Alice in Wonderland*. "You made it, sweetheart! You are officially in ODP!"

I squealed and jumped into Dad's arms. This was my dream come true. Dad was right—his news revived me. First, I would call Rachel with the news. Then, I would take two Tylenol and celebrate big time!

CHAPTER THREE
EVENING BEFORE
THE BEGINNING OF THE END

As our team ran out onto the field the night of the big championship game at Atlanta's Talmage-Mitchell Stadium, everyone in the stands who were East Lake High supporters, jumped to their feet and screamed "Go Bombers!" The sound reverberated throughout the stadium. My arms broke out in goose bumps from an adrenaline rush.

My best friend and teammate, Rachel, ran up and pounded my back. "Look at that mob of people!" she screamed in my ear over the roar of the crowd. I could barely hear her.

Shaking my head, I tried to rub away the annoying ache in my shoulder. The stadium was packed, like it was Homecoming Football Weekend. "Coach says it's the largest crowd he's ever seen for the final playoff," I screamed back.

Rachel nudged me with her hip. "Right! They came to see the East Lake Bombers win the state championship. They know we're going to win because you, Lindsey Anderson, are the real Bomb!"

I faced my BFF head on. "No one player can win a game. It takes a team. We're a team."

"Yeah, yeah, I get it! And you're the real Bomb because not just anybody gets into the ODP." She smirked.

I growled. "That doesn't mean anything as far as this game goes. Why are we gonna win tonight?"

We pounded our fists in the air and screamed, "We're the East Lake Bombers! We're the BEST!"

·   ·   ·   ·

From the first minute of play, I focused on getting the ball down the field, past the Excalibur goalkeeper and into the back net. I tried to shake off an overall feeling of body fatigue. We had ended last night's birthday celebration early, so I could have eight hours of sleep. But I didn't wake up feeling all that energetic.

Meanwhile, the Excalibur players were on top of their game. No surprise there. They were the No. 1 ranked team and defending state champions. Still, I knew we could beat them, and early on we scored the first point.

At halftime, it was still 1-0. Coach Burdine was all smiles, but he reminded us the game wasn't over. "Excalibur will come back with blood in their eye." He wasn't kidding about blood in their eye. I don't know what the Excalibur coach told his team, but they managed to bounce a ball into the net almost immediately, tying the score 1-1.

"Holy crap!" I screamed, watching the Excalibur players jubilantly jumping up and down. I shook my head in disgust and huddled around my teammates. "Come on, team! Don't give up!

We can beat them." There was no freaking way we were losing tonight.

It was a long, hard-fought second half. The Excalibur players were relentless. We couldn't get the ball anywhere close to the goal box. Time was running out for us to score. With everyone exhausted, we were down to the final seconds of the game. The crowd was screaming so loud in the stands I could feel the ground vibrating beneath my feet. Excalibur had won the championship the past three years. It was our turn to pull off a victory. We couldn't let it slip away. This was my last game as an East Lake Bomber. I'd never have another chance.

Taking a deep breath, I thought of my mom. A former soccer star herself, she had introduced me to the game when I was six. If she hadn't died, she'd be in the stands next to Dad. "This is for you, Mom!" I screamed. Then I stole the ball away from an Excalibur player, knocking her to the ground.

Ignoring this weird tightness across my chest, I kicked the ball to Rachel and sprinted toward the goal as fast as I could. Rachel kicked it back to me. My heart was beating so fast, it felt like it was going to leap out of my chest. Catching the Excalibur goalkeeper off-guard, I made my play. She lunged for the ball, but missed. Even before the referee's whistle blew three times, I knew we'd won, 2-1!

The East Lake Bombers screamed and raised their arms in victory. We were triumphant! My ears hurt from the roar that went up in the stands. It was worse than any rock concert. I ran toward Rachel and my teammates, gasping for breath. As they pulled me to their shoulders, my scream strangled in my throat. A pain began deep inside my chest—like someone with cleats was standing on it. Tears blurred my vision.

Then I was toppling forward. A sea of hands grabbed for me. When I hit the ground, I could smell crushed grass and trampled dirt. Rachel's worried face loomed over mine, her mouth opening and closing, but I couldn't hear what she was saying. In slow motion, my teammates pulled back and Dad knelt beside me, touching my face and squeezing my hand. I could feel the warmth of his love. Was I dying? No, that couldn't be. I was too young. My whole life lay ahead of me. I had big plans for the rest of my life. But a cold numbness spread upwards from my toes, and I drifted away into total darkness.

CHAPTER FOUR
TOTAL CONFUSION

In my dream, the darkness slowly turns to light. What a great dream! The kind you want to last forever. I sigh blissfully. I'm alive and feeling good. Warm sun rays stroke my face, and a gentle breeze tousles my hair as I kick the winning goal. Everyone is yelling my name. "Lindsey, Lindsey, Lindsey!" Victory is mine. Then suddenly I'm flying and floating overhead through cool, misty clouds. I'm full of wonder and elation. No fear or terror. I enjoy the moment.

In the distance, I heard soothing voices that gradually grew louder and increasingly persistent.

"Annabeth, this is Dr. Steve Hopkins. Can you hear me?"

Annabeth? Who is Annabeth? Awakened from my soothing dream, I felt annoyance at the intruder's voice. I frowned and opened my eyes reluctantly. A white-haired, plump-faced nurse hovered over me. Next to her stood a familiar figure in a white lab coat—a tall, thin man in his early forties with a Lance Armstrong haircut and a Grecian nose.

Who did he say he was? Dr. Hopkins? Wait. I knew that name <u>and</u> that face. He had visited my human biology class and showed us how to figure out our blood type. What was he doing in my nightmare?

Trying to sit up made me hurt all over. Like an 18-wheeler had run over me twice. When I tried to speak, my mouth didn't work.

Dr. Hopkins gently touched my shoulder. "Take it easy. You need to rest."

And then I remembered more. His obnoxious child-prodigy son Justin was in my human biology class. The cherub-faced brat with the fly-away blond hair. Beloved by his teachers and hated by me. Because he totally annoyed me. Oh, how he loved to annoy me. He claimed I was the love of his life and did not hesitate to let everyone at East Lake High know how he felt. Did he really think that any high school senior would give a 15-year-old child genius a second look? Even one who had been offered a full scholarship to M.I.T., Harvard, Princeton, and Yale?

Dr. Hopkins leaned over my face. "The nurse found you unconscious on the floor."

The vision of the haunted face in the mirror—the one that wasn't mine—flashed in front of me.

"You have a serious concussion," he said. "You almost died in the ER."

My heart flopped and started to race.

"You're lucky to be alive. Please, if you need to get up, use your call button. Do you know where you are?"

"Hospital," I whispered hoarsely. But how did I end up here, and why was I not myself today? I swallowed hard. Funny how I could remember every annoying detail about Justin, but I couldn't remember how I ended up in the hospital.

"Excellent!" Dr. Hopkins patted my hand. "What's your name?"

I frowned. My brain felt groggy. My name? I knew it earlier. My friends had shouted it in my soccer dream. I closed my eyes.

"Take your time, you'll get it," Dr. Hopkins said.

I relaxed my face as the name formed in my mouth. "Lindsey . . . Lindsey Anderson." I jumped at the sound of my voice, which still didn't sound like mine. The nurse and doctor exchanged strange looks.

Dr. Hopkins gave me a quick nod. "You're doing fine. Just lie there and get some rest. It's not unusual after a concussion to experience confusion, headache, nausea, blurred vision, and memory loss."

Yeah. All of the above. *So, a concussion is my problem?* Relief flooded over me. While being carried across the field, I must have fallen and landed on my head. My brain was fried. No wonder I didn't look like myself. I held out my arm with the splint. "What happened to my arm?"

"You don't remember?"

I shook my head.

Dr. Hopkins gently touched my good arm. "This bone here—your radius—is fractured."

That must have been some fall, I thought. "And here?" I pointed to the bandage around my ribs.

"A fractured rib."

"And my forehead?"

"A small cut. Four stitches." He reached for my hand and gave it a squeeze. "Don't worry. You're going to be fine in a few days. By the way, your friend is very anxious to see you. Would you like to see her?"

"Oh, yes, please!" It was about time Rachel showed up. I wanted Dad, but I would settle for my best friend. Dad would be here soon.

"The nurse will tell her you're awake. But it will have to be a short visit this time, because you need to rest." He and the nurse started toward the door.

"Thank you, Dr. Hopkins." He smiled as he shut the door behind him. I couldn't wait to see Rachel. She could fill me in on all the details. Rachel would laugh herself silly when I told her my concussion was so bad, I actually thought I was in somebody else's body. I yawned. I couldn't believe how tired I was. My eyelids closed and I faded away.

•   •   •   •   •

When I woke up—two hours later, according to the wall clock— my head still hurt, but it felt less overstuffed. I was disappointed that Rachel and Dad weren't here. I sat up slowly. The dizziness wasn't too bad this time, and the nausea had gone away. I reached for the phone on the bedside table and pulled it into my lap. Lifting the receiver to my ear, I dialed Dad's cell phone number. It rang four times before Dad's voice mail kicked in. "You have reached the voice mail of Dr. Reginald Anderson. I'm sorry I'm not here to take your call. Please leave your name and number, and I will get back to you. Have a good day. Beep!"

"Uh—Dad—it's me. Uh—I don't know what's going on. I woke up in the hospital. Where are you? Call me. Love you." I hung up. I didn't understand. Where could Dad be? I fought down a lump in my throat. I knew there was a good reason he wasn't here. And where was Rachel? She should be here by now, too.

While I was feeling sorry for myself, a knock sounded on the door. I looked up, expecting to see Rachel. Instead, a young teenage girl nervously twisting a frizzy, henna-dyed curl around short, pudgy fingers hesitantly entered the room. *Holy crap!* E-ew! As she edged closer to my bed, her body odor was overwhelming. She smelled worse than a pile of dirty soccer uniforms after a game. And her outfit was strictly early Salvation Army—peasant blouse, cheap costume jewelry, Spandex leopard-print mini-skirt, thigh-high faux-crocodile boots. Not only did I not know her, but I didn't want to know her.

Her chubby-cheeked face didn't look familiar, but when our eyes met, she smiled broadly, exposing a mouthful of teeth behind full, chocolate-brown lips. She scurried toward me—like I was her long-lost best friend. She literally leaped on the bed and tried to hug me. "Annabeth! You're alive!" Then she wiggled her butt and squealed so high-pitched my ears hurt.

I pushed her back. "Stop! You're hurting me."

The smile left her face, as she backed off the bed. "Chill out! Excuse me for caring about you, girlfriend." She tilted her head slightly and popped her gum. "Yo, Annabeth. You look pretty awful. Are you in a lot of pain?" She shook her head and made some sort of sympathetic sounds.

Annabeth? Why did everyone call me Annabeth? "Who *are* you?" My tongue felt ten sizes too big for my mouth, and I didn't have enough spit to swallow. What I would give for a can of Cherry Coke.

"Damn, girlfriend. What's up with you? It's me, Neeley."

She moved her face within an inch of mine. Her breath smelled like Juicy Fruit gum. And her nose was pierced. Double e-ew! Didn't her nose hurt if she had to blow it? "I don't know you." I tried to clear my throat. Why did my voice sound so weird?

"Shut up! You're freaking me out!" She took a step back. "That hottie doctor say you got a concussion. That's just a fancified word for knocked in the head. Did that flatten out your memory banks or something?"

"I've never seen you before." If I passed her on the street, I would probably clutch my purse tighter. I instantly hoped my wallet was in a safe place. Was this the "friend" Dr. Hopkins said was waiting to see me? Not Rachel? I looked down at the hands that didn't look like mine. This was no hallucination brought on by a concussion.

"Come on, Annabeth, we done been roommates for nearly a year. What's wrong with you, girl?"

My head started to throb, again. *What? Did she say we lived together?* I would sooner share a room with my Aunt Clementine, who whistled through her nose and smelled like cat food. "I am *not* who you think I am." But if I wasn't myself . . . if the girl in the mirror wasn't me . . . then I had to be in somebody else's body. It was basic logic. My scalp prickled. My brain shut down for several seconds, then I dismissed the thought. It was totally too crazy to deal with. I was obviously not in my right mind. I was not myself today.

The girl giggled, stood up, and tugged on her tight mini-skirt. "Annabeth, you're teasing me, right?" She propped her right foot on my bed and scratched her inner thigh. *Did that boot really have a 6-inch stiletto heel?*

She reminded me of the teenage girls Rachel and I saw on the evening news last month. Over 30 underage girls had been rescued in Metro Atlanta after a crackdown on child sex trafficking. We were like totally shocked to see how young they were. We had asked ourselves if it were possible that our own lives could ever get so bad that we'd end up like them? Was it possible that we could ever become sex trafficking victims?

"How old are you?" I asked. She looked like a 12-year-old with her face painted for a dance recital or a school production.

The girl snatched her foot off my bed. "Fourteen. Same as you, girlfriend." She leaned over into my personal space, smacking and popping her Juicy Fruit gum. "Don't you remember nothing?"

She was not the kind of person I would forget. My volunteer group mentored young teens at the Girls Club downtown. None of them were this obnoxious.

"C'mon, you know me, Annabeth. Don't tease me. We're best friends." She straightened up, hands on hips.

"I am Lindsey Anderson. Let me assure you, we are not best friends." The very thought made my stomach hurt worse. Perish the thought that I could ever be best friends with the likes of her. No way would that ever happen! Not the daughter of the Bosch Research Institute director; not the co-captain of the East Lake High School soccer team.

"Are you shitting me, Annabeth? Didn't I take care of you when you had the flu and was throwing up all over everywhere? And who pierced your nipple? Who else would have done that for free, huh?"

Holy crap! Frantically, I peered down the neck of my hospital gown and groaned. My C-cup breasts were gone—shrunk down to a pair of A-cup bee stings. I sucked in my breath at the sight of a silver hoop piercing my right nipple. As soon as I got over this feeling of disgust, I would pull it out.

Neeley smirked. "So don't try and tell me you ain't Annabeth Shepard. Don't mess with me." She reached down into her bra and pulled out a photo. "Here. You don't believe me? Look at this." She held out a wrinkled photo.

My hand trembled. I didn't want to touch it, but that traitorous right hand reached out and grabbed it anyway. I was too terrified to look. I gasped and dropped it.

Neeley shook her head, picked it up off the floor, and placed it on the nightstand. Two laughing teenage girls—looking like BFF—stared back at me. They had their arms around each other's shoulders. One girl was Neeley. The other, a cleaned-up version of the girl I had seen in the mirror—Annabeth. There it was. Full-color proof that I was trapped in Annabeth's body. It felt like ice water was flowing through my veins. Swallowing a scream, I fell back against the pillow and covered my mouth.

Neeley shook one chubby finger in my face. "You the one who stole Tony's drug money. You said we was gonna get away from him and start a new life together. You promised me, remember?"

A little pain started in my brain, right between my eyes. I was borderline hysterical. "Why would I steal his money?" My weird voice rose in pitch. I'd watched enough *FBI* and *Hawaii 5-0* to know that only idiots came between drug dealers and their money.

"Because we hate our lives!" Neeley threw her hands up in the air. "We do all the work, and Tony takes all our money. Not to mention the abuse we have to deal with. Remember?"

I rubbed the bridge of my nose. "Look here, Neeley, I don't know what you're talking about." And I didn't want to know either. The nervous fluttering in my abdomen was turning into violent cramps. "Please, you keep the money and have a good life." I had enough problems to deal with now; I didn't need to worry about anything else.

"I wish that was possible, but how can I? Tony and his goon be looking for both of us? Look at yourself, Annabeth! He nearly killed you. That's why you don't remember a freaking thing." Neeley jutted out her lower lip into a pout. "Anyways, I don't know where the money's at. You the one who hid it. That's why you lying there half-dead and not me."

"ME?" *Holy crap!* This girl was scaring me worse than a brain-eating zombie. How could I believe anything she said? She was nothing but a teenage hooker. Doing who knows what with strange men for money or drugs. I wrapped my arms around myself to calm my shaking body. She was probably harboring a sexual disease or body lice or something worse. I didn't see how I could help her.

Neeley poked a pudgy finger into my shoulder. "You might not freaking care now, but you better be getting outta this place real soon. We gotta get that money and leave town before Tony finds us, again. 'Cause if he does, girlfriend, he's gonna kill us both."

I wanted Neeley out of my room. I needed space to figure this out. If I were in Annabeth's body, then it stood to reason that Annabeth had to be in my body. A coldness seeped into the pit of my stomach. That meant my body was in this hospital, too. I sat up straight in bed with one thought racing through my mind. I couldn't lie here and do nothing. I had to find Dad. Even if it meant ripping the IV out of my arm and jumping out the window.

CHAPTER FIVE
TAKING CONTROL

I was trying to get Neeley to leave when the door jerked open. A man wearing a baggy, wrinkled suit and carrying a well-worn black fedora hat stepped quietly into the room.

Neeley squealed. It wasn't a happy, excited squeal.

"Miss Hill?" the man called out, as she backed away from him.

I gasped. Could this be Tony? The man Neeley was talking about? Was he here to kill us? But he didn't look like any drug dealer I'd seen on TV. More like one of those old, retired guys you see sitting on benches in Piedmont Park.

"Remember me?" He held up a badge in front of Neeley. "Lieutenant Richards, Atlanta P.D. You left before we were finished talking." He took a step in her direction, but Neeley bolted for the door, bumping into the nurse.

The nurse glared at the police detective, as Neeley ran out of the room. "Sir, I told you earlier that you can't be in here. The doctor said . . ."

But the man waved his hat dismissively at the nurse and was standing at the edge of my bed before she could finish her sentence. He leaned over me, like he needed to get a closer look at my face. His face was so close, I could see the large pores and blackheads on his huge, potato nose, and smell the stale cigarette smoke that stunk up his clothes. This hospital room was attracting weird characters like nails to a magnet. I was beginning to feel like Alice-down-the-rabbit-hole.

With his fingers, the man raked greasy locks of dark gray and black hair off his lined forehead. "Miss, I'm Detective Lieutenant Richards, Atlanta PD. If you feel up to it, I'd like to ask you a few questions."

"Sir, you have to leave," the nurse insisted.

He turned and glared at the nurse. "Lady, will you please let me do my job? Her life could be in danger." The detective twisted his hat in his hands. "And yours, too."

Holy crap! My life could be in danger? I cringed and pulled the sheet up to my chin.

The nurse chewed her bottom lip and shook a finger at him. "Two minutes." She turned her back and began writing on my chart.

"Thanks." He turned back to me. "Okay, Miss, are you up for questions?"

"I think so." At least I remembered my name. Maybe not who I was now or why I wasn't me anymore, but I knew where I was and that my life was in jeopardy.

He pulled out a small notebook and pen. "Tell me what happened last night."

"I kicked the winning goal for the Women's Soccer State Championship, then . . ." I closed my eyes and pictured me kicking the ball. "Things get a little fuzzy after that. Everyone was screaming." I opened my eyes. "I think maybe I fell on my head, but I'm not sure. Have you talked to any of my teammates yet?"

The detective stared at me like I just told him I was a unicorn in another life. He turned to the nurse. "Isn't this the assault victim?"

The nurse motioned him towards the door. The detective followed her, never taking his eyes off mine. As they both left the room, I noticed Dr. Hopkins standing in the doorway, staring at me.

"What are you looking at?" I asked him. The words came out strange sounding, and my whole body started shaking uncontrollably.

Dr. Hopkins walked over to my bed. "You mean 'who,' don't you? Who are you? You had no ID on you when you arrived in ER. Your friend gave us your name. Do you have parents we can call?"

"Call my d-d-dad." Suddenly my teeth began to chatter. "Wha-a-at's wrr-ong with me?"

"Withdrawal symptoms," he answered matter-of-factly.

What was he talking about? "Withdrawal from what?"

"Heroin."

"I don't do drugs!" But I did remember reading a pamphlet about drug withdrawal in the school counselor's office, and chills and cramps were definitely symptoms. My mind whirled. *Holy crap!*

"The lab reports indicate otherwise."

"I'm . . . no . . . addict." But my whole body shivered and ached.

"Then what's this?" he asked, turning over my skinny left arm—the one that didn't belong to me—and exposing needle tracks inside my elbow.

"But that's not my arm," I protested, pulling it away from his grip. The rest of my words died in my throat. How could I explain this? The arm was attached to my body—the body that didn't belong to me either. This could not be happening to me. This was not possible. I could not be a drug-addicted teenage hooker.

"In addition to methadone for your drug addiction, I've ordered intravenous antibiotics to clear up your STDs." He paused. "That's sexually transmitted disease."

Each word struck like a punch to the gut. "*Holy crap!*" I was probably one of the few virgins left at East Lake High. The thought of this body having sex with strange men off the street—unprotected sex—was sickening. I almost gagged.

Dr. Hopkins pulled a chair over to my bed and sat down. "Annabeth, it's normal under the circumstances for you to be confused," he said, his voice full of concern. "Your brain needs time to heal. I want to help you. After talking to your friend and looking over your chart, I suspect that you ran away from home and got caught up in a sex trafficking operation. More than half of the homeless youth in metro Atlanta have been caught up in human trafficking." He reached over and squeezed my hand. "Let me call your parents, Annabeth. Let me help you get your life back before it's too late."

Well, yeah! I wanted to get my life back, too. My brain pulsed and pounded like it was in overdrive. How I wished Dr. Hopkins could help me do this. But I didn't see how I could make him understand. "My name . . ." I took a deep breath. ". . . is not Annabeth."

"Your friend says it is."

"I'm telling you, she's not my friend." My body continued to shake beyond my control. I didn't know if I could go on. Dad had always been my rock. He was always there for me, solving any problems too big for me.

Dr. Hopkins fingered the photo on the nightstand. "Whatever you say."

I glanced at the photo of Neeley and Annabeth. A chill ran up my spine and my hands trembled. *Holy crap!* I was in serious trouble. I grabbed Dr. Hopkins' hand. "Please," I begged, "find my dad."

He looked relieved. "Yes, I want to do that. Who is he? How can I reach him?" Dr. Hopkins pulled out a small black notebook and a pen.

Just then the nurse entered the room carrying a hypodermic and injected the contents into my IV. "This methadone will help with your drug withdrawal symptoms," she said.

I closed my eyes. I could actually feel the drug speeding through my veins. My brain raced, sifting through everything I knew, and what I didn't. While Dr. Hopkins was finding Dad, I was going to get out of this room and find my body. "Dr. Reginald Anderson."

Dr. Hopkins jumped out of his seat. "What was that?"

"My dad. Reginald Anderson."

"Impossible! I know Dr. Anderson. His daughter Lindsey was in my son's class. I've met her, and it's not possible that you're Lindsey Anderson!" He backed toward the door. "You're not Lindsey Anderson!"

Totally shocked at his outburst, I watched an angry Dr. Hopkins leave the room, slamming the door shut behind him. *Holy crap!* He knows my dad. And he remembers meeting me when he came to my human biology class. I had to talk to Dad. I pulled the phone into my lap, lifted the receiver, and punched in my home number. After the second ring, I heard my dad's voice. "Hello?" He sounded hoarse, tired and sad, like when Mom died.

I gripped the receiver tightly. "Dad?"

"You must have the wrong number."

"No, it's me . . . Lindsey."

The silence that followed was so long, I thought he had hung up. "Who?"

"Your daughter, Lindsey. Dad, I'm in St. Mary's. Something terrible has happened to . . ." The line went dead.

My eyes stung as they filled with tears. I couldn't believe my own dad hung up on me. I wiped my eyes with the back of my hand and picked up the receiver, again. This time I called Dad's cell phone. It was on him at all times.

"Hello?" His voice sounded wary and cautious.

"Don't hang up. Please! I need help!"

"You most certainly do, young lady. You are one sick individual. Don't call here, again!" He disconnected.

I slowly dropped the receiver into the cradle. A sob escaped from my throat. I wanted to scream and break something, but that would only get me a knock-out shot or a straitjacket or both. I chewed my lower lip. Dad wasn't going to rescue me this time. Time to move on to Plan B and find my body myself. It had to be in this hospital somewhere.

Kicking off the covers, I dangled my legs over the side of the bed. My head still hurt and I felt a little bit dizzy. The cramping in my stomach was mostly gone, but I had some achiness in one arm, and my fractured rib hurt when I breathed. Shoot, I'd felt a whole lot worse after a soccer game.

I grabbed a thin cotton robe off the end of my bed and slipped it on. Thank goodness it would cover my butt in the back. I almost skipped the slippers, but after thinking about what could be on a hospital floor, I changed my mind. I grabbed the IV stand and stood up unsteadily. I took one step and didn't pass out. I could do this.

No one was in the hall except a young female volunteer pushing a cart full of magazines. She smiled at me like seeing me was the best thing that had happened to her today. "Hello, how are you?"

I wanted to say: I've been beaten to a bloody pulp, I hurt all over, and I woke up this morning in the body of a drug-addicted teenage hooker. Instead, I said, "Fine, thank you." *If people don't really want to know how you are, why do they ask?*

The volunteer stopped her cart next to me. "I have the new issue of *Teen Beat* magazine here. Want me to leave it in your room?"

"Thank you, but I'm almost totally blind."

Her smile faded. "Oh . . . I'm so sorry. Is there something else I can get for you?"

I pushed my IV tree past her. "Thanks, but I'm just out for a walk." I turned the corner, out of her view.

I read every name on every door on the fourth floor and peeked in every room. I did not see my name or my body. By the time I returned to my room, I was exhausted, and my headache was making the top of my head throb. I pushed open my door and halted in my tracks.

CHAPTER SIX
REALITY CHECK

A thin, white-haired guy sat beside my bed. He had a Hollywood tan, a smooth complexion, a pointy nose, and no lips. I glanced from his pink shirt and purple tie to the hospital file teetering on his knees, and coughed as an overpowering scent of lavender tickled the back of my throat.

"Oh, you're back," he said. "Please join me."

"Who are you?" I sat down gingerly on the edge of my bed.

"I'm Dr. Bill Epting. Dr. Hopkins asked me to stop by and chat with you."

"Why?"

"He's worried about you. He thought that I might be able to help you with your—uh—problems."

He had a smile like Bruce, that predator shark in the *Nemo* movie. "What kind of doctor are you?" Maybe he specialized in drug addiction cases.

"A staff psychologist for St. Mary's."

If that wasn't just great. I tell them I'm not Annabeth and now, they think I need a shrink. "I'm not crazy." Although at the moment I was beginning to have my doubts. Like maybe I really was this Annabeth person. Like maybe I was hallucinating about ever being Lindsey Anderson. I didn't see how that was possible. But how could being in somebody else's body be scientifically possible? All of this made my head hurt even worse.

Dr. Epting grinned. "No one said you were. I'm only here to evaluate the possibility of trauma-induced delusions."

Trauma-induced delusions? My dad said Aunt Clementine was delusional because she talked to her dead husband, Uncle Ernie. I just thought she was old.

"ER patients frequently have brain injuries that can cause amnesia or cognitive impairment."

I rubbed my head where the pain seemed to be centered.

Dr. Epting touched the photo on my nightstand and smiled. "What a nice photo, Annabeth. Is this your friend?"

My stomach tightened into a knot. "For the record, she is not my friend, and I'm not Annabeth. I'm Lindsey Anderson."

He scribbled something down in his notes. Probably that I was hostile.

"I see . . . hmmm . . . well . . . my information indicates that you're Annabeth Shepard. That you were physically attacked and beaten."

I shook my head. "No, I'm pretty sure I'm Lindsey Anderson, high school soccer star."

Dr. Epting's pale, gray eyes pierced mine, but I couldn't turn away from his gaze. It was creepy, like he was trying to read my mind. He looked down and thumbed through the pages in his file, picking up one. "This police report says otherwise."

My head started to pound. "I don't care what the report says. Something happened to me on the soccer field last night. Something that put me into Annabeth's body."

Dr. Epting jumped slightly and stared at me long and hard. His eyes narrowed. I recognized that look. He was considering carefully what to say next. It's the same look Dad gives me when I say or ask something dumb, like "Why does it matter if his parents won't be home during his party?"

The doctor took a deep breath. "This mistaken identity must be terribly confusing for you."

I sighed. Was I just going to shut up and give up? Or was I going to tell him everything? Like I was living that old Disney movie *Freaky Friday?* Except in real life, swapping bodies didn't happen, and if it did, it certainly wouldn't be a comedy.

I continued to stare at him in silence, while I thought about what I was going to say. Why wouldn't anyone believe me? But let's face it: if anybody told me this body-swapping story, I wouldn't believe them either. I was living the nightmare, and I didn't believe it. Still, he was a psychologist. He talked to crazy people all the time.

I swallowed hard and fought down the panic. "Dr. Epting—" My hands shook. I whispered, causing him to lean forward to hear me. "I don't look like myself. I'm not myself today. This isn't my body." I shoved my hands close to his face. "Seriously, these are not my hands. Look at the nails and cuticles. These hands have never had a manicure." I touched my cheek. "And this face? It isn't mine, either." My voice cracked. "Do you understand? I woke up in a piece of crap body that I've never seen before." A sob escaped from my throat.

Dr. Epting leaned back in his chair, taking a quick glance at his notes. "Let's make sure I understand you correctly: You woke up this morning in a body that isn't yours?"

Shaking all over, my teeth chattering, I took a deep breath. "It's like I'm in a horror movie. This can't be real or even possible." I handed him the photo of Neeley and Annabeth and tapped on it with my finger. "Can't you see that this body looks like the girl in the photo? I look like Annabeth Shepard."

Dr. Epting nodded and scribbled something down. "Yes, the resemblance is remarkable."

"Yes, but you don't understand." I touched my hands to my chest. "If I'm Lindsey Anderson, and I'm in Annabeth Shepard's body, then somewhere in this hospital is my body with Annabeth inside." I wiped my nose, again.

Dr. Epting cocked his head and cleared his throat. "Yes, that is a logical thought process." He wrote more words.

"I've looked in every room on this floor, and I can't find myself." I took a deep breath, fighting down a lump in my throat. "I need to find me, don't you understand? I'm not myself today. Graduation is coming up, and I don't want to march down the aisle and get my diploma in this body. And it isn't just graduation at stake here, but the rest of my life. I have my full-ride soccer scholarship to Stanford. And one day, I hope to play on the USA Women's Soccer Team at the World Olympics."

Dr. Epting looked up from his notes. "I most definitely understand your problem, and I think that if we work together, we can remedy the situation."

"Oh, thank you, Dr. Epting." I sighed. "The sooner we straighten this out, the better. I have finals to study for, two papers to finish, and I'm heading up the committee for the Great Graduation Bash."

He tapped his pen on his chin. "Just a few more questions and we'll be finished. Could you please give me the names of your parents?"

"Winifred and Reginald Anderson, but my mom died when I was in sixth grade."

He paused, the pen hovering in mid-air over his writing pad. "Dr. Reginald Anderson on the hospital board? The director of the Bosch Research Institute?"

"Do you know my dad?" I was suddenly flooded with relief and hope. "Don't you think he's awesome? A brilliant scientist and a generous philanthropist. Did you see his interview last month with David Muir?"

"Yes, I certainly did." Dr. Epting wiped his face with a lavender handkerchief. "Is he—uh—aware of the situation here?"

"I don't know. I've tried to reach him." He didn't need to know that Dad refused to talk to me. "Wherever he is, whatever he's doing that prevents him from being here with me, I know it's very important." Once Dad realized what was going on, he'd straighten everything out.

Dr. Epting slammed the file shut and stood up. "Please excuse me. I—uh—need to meet with someone now, but we'll chat more later."

Before I could open my mouth, he was out the door. Which was fine by me. I had work to do. That dirty, little, body-snatching Annabeth was somewhere, surrounded by my sympathetic, loving friends and family, while I was stuck with her crappy body, her clingy, best friend, and a murderous drug dealer out for revenge.

Wishing I had a Cherry Coke because my mouth felt dry, like I'd been wandering across Death Valley, I reached for a water glass and brushed my hand against the telephone. Can you say patient information? They would know where Lindsey Anderson was. Why didn't I think of this sooner? I lifted up the receiver and pressed zero.

"St. Mary's. How may I direct your call?"

"Patient information, please." I waited for the connection. I couldn't wait to get Annabeth on the phone and give her a piece of my mind. No, that wouldn't work. I would get her room number and confront her in person. Make her admit she was in my body.

"Patient information."

"Yes, could you please tell me what room Lindsey Anderson is in?" I listened to the faint clicking of computer keys.

"I'm sorry, but I show no one by that name admitted to St. Mary's."

I dropped the receiver. If my body wasn't here, where was it? Then I relaxed. Of course, I had been released from the hospital. I dialed my home number. The phone rang four times.

"Hel-lo?" My father sounded like he had been asleep.

"Dad?" I willed myself not to get hysterical.

"Who is this?"

I took a deep breath. "Lindsey."

He didn't respond, but he didn't hang up. I could hear him breathing.

"I love you, Dad. You have to help me."

He still said nothing.

"Dad, I know that you took me home from the hospital today. Haven't you noticed that I'm not myself? It's because it's not me. It's a teenage hooker in my body, and I'm here at the hospital in hers. Let me speak to her." Something thudded on the other end. "Dad, don't hang up." I heard a strangled noise.

Fear spread through my body, as a horrific thought suddenly crossed my mind. I was right all along. Annabeth liked my body, my dad, my best friend, and my entire life. Annabeth didn't want her body back. She didn't want to be a sex trafficking victim, anymore. She didn't want to be roommates with Neeley Hill. She didn't want to worry about getting murdered. Annabeth knew she was better off in my body. I was totally screwed.

"Listen to me, young lady." Dad's voice sounded like he was border-line exploding. "I do not know what game you're playing. My daughter isn't here. Do you understand? She's never coming home, again. My daughter is dead!" He hung up.

I sat back totally confused. *My body was like dead-dead?* As in Annabeth was not walking around in it? A sharp, cold tremor of pain pierced the middle of my abdomen, and I thought I would throw up. I knew of only one place where my body could be.

· · · · ·

After they removed my dinner tray, I told the nurse I was taking a walk. I went for a walk all right. Straight into the elevator and down to the basement. When the doors opened, the hallway was deathly quiet and empty. The only sounds came from my IV tree as I pushed it out of the elevator. A sign indicated equipment storage and patient records archives were to the right; I went left.

I kept expecting the bright lights overhead to blink and go out, followed by some really creepy music, like in the horror movies just before the monster kills his next victim. Every 10 feet or so I stopped and listened for footsteps or somebody breathing heavy. Nothing.

I kept going, even though my brain was screaming, "Lindsey, you idiot, are you crazy?" You know how the girl in the horror movie hears a crash on the other side of the door and then opens it? You know the monster is on the other side waiting for her. Why doesn't she know it? I bit my knuckles. "Don't do it, Lindsey!" But I know why the girl opens that door every time. It's like she's been hypnotized. I knew I shouldn't be doing this, but I couldn't help myself.

I rounded another corner and there it was in front of me. Two frosted glass sliding doors lettered "St. Mary's Hospital Morgue." The doors slid open as I approached. Like the front door of Dracula's Castle slowly squeaking open, and nobody's there. Nobody was here, either. But I saw another door about 10 feet away. I took a deep breath. There was no turning back now.

I pressed a buzzer button to the side of the door and waited. Would anyone be here this time of night? And if so, what would I say?

It seemed like forever before I heard footsteps on the other side of the door, which was opened by a young man with a boyish face and very short black hair. He wore blue hospital scrubs with an ID badge carrying his photo and name: Fleming Moore, Technician. He seemed as surprised to see me as I was to see him. I guess with my bruised, swollen face and bandages—not to mention the patient gown and robe and IV tree—I was not the typical visitor to the hospital morgue. Plus, I was still breathing.

He looked up and down the hall to see if I were alone. He cocked his head and frowned. "Can I help you?"

I sighed. "I hope so, Fleming." I added a tremor to my voice, which wasn't hard since I was kind of stressing out at this point. "I'm—" I swallowed hard. "Uh—I'm Annabeth Shephard. My friend and I came into the ER last night. A terrible accident. I'm going to be okay, but my friend—uh—she died."

Fleming stepped back and opened the door all the way. "I'm so sorry. What can I do to help?"

I nudged the IV tree closer to him and the door. "I—uh—need to see my friend. To say good-bye."

"Oh." He blinked. "I don't know about that. I can't let just anyone in here without permission." He started closing the door in my face.

I let out a whimper. "Oh, please Fleming! A sob escaped my throat. "She was my best friend forever." Then I scrunched up my face and let a few tears run down my cheeks.

Fleming leaped over to me, patting my shoulder. "Hey, it's okay. Please, don't cry." He looked up and down the hall, again. Then he put his arm around me and helped me through the doorway. The door clicked shut behind us.

He rubbed his forehead. "I could get into trouble for this, but if you'll stop crying, I'll try and locate your friend, and maybe you can see her for just a few minutes."

I wiped my nose on the sleeve of my robe. "I wouldn't want you to lose your job or anything." I widened my eyes and fluttered my lashes. If Annabeth was making money as a hooker, there had to be something appealing about her.

Fleming's face turned pink. He sat down in front of a flat-screen monitor. "Not too many people come down here after hours."

Apparently not. *Forge of Empires* filled the screen of his iPad, and a bowl of popcorn was almost empty.

He grinned up at me sheepishly and turned off his iPad. "Yeah, it can get pretty quiet and boring down here in the evenings. But you never know when someone will stop by. So, what's the name of your friend?"

I rubbed my finger back and forth over the tattoo. "Lindsey Anderson."

He nodded and keystroked in the name.

I watched my name flash onto the monitor.

Fleming hit "Enter." In seconds, "Drawer 3127" appeared. With a pencil, he jotted the number on a piece of paper and jumped to his feet. He opened the door and pointed down the hall. "Down there on your left. Follow me."

•   •   •   •   •

The room we entered looked like the typical morgue you see on TV shows, except there were no bodies lying out on stainless steel tables. Everything was shiny and spotless, just like in the OR. I detected a faint odor of disinfectant, but nothing that smelled of rotting corpses. One entire wall of the room consisted of stainless steel drawers. A giant filing cabinet.

I followed Fleming to this wall. He double-checked the number on his paper and stopped with his hand on the handle of one of the drawers. My knees began to feel rubbery, but I didn't see any place to sit.

Fleming looked at me. "Are you ready?"

I nodded, chewed my lower lip, and breathed deeply several times. "I'm ready," I whispered.

Fleming pulled out the drawer part way, showing a black body bag.

As I edged closer to Fleming, he pulled down the zipper, exposing the face and shoulders of a female body. With my face. It was definitely me. My stomach lurched, and I gasped. I couldn't get my breath.

Fleming's eyes widened, and I could see the panic in his face. "Oh, please, don't faint." He grabbed my shoulders tightly, as though to hold me up in case I did.

It was probably a good thing. I could feel my legs buckling, as I stared down at my damp auburn-red hair, brushed back from my face. I looked peacefully asleep, but my skin color was on the grayish side. I reached out and touched my face and jumped at the coldness.

"Sorry about your loss," Fleming said, still gripping me tightly. "Had you known her long?"

"Since she was born," I answered softly. "We were best friends." I sighed. *Okay, Lindsey, here I am and there you are. Now what?* I placed one hand on either side of the body's face and closed my eyes. *God are you listening? Something seriously wrong is going on down here.* I sighed softly. Dad and I had stopped going to church after Mom died. But even though I was angry at God for many years after her death, I still found myself praying to God on occasion.

So, God, if you're up there listening, this is me, Lindsey. You put me in this hooker's body, for whatever reason. Now I'm ready to get my birth body back. If you can straighten out this mess, I promise to be the best daughter ever, go to church every Sunday, read the daily devotion, and help out everyone who is not as blessed as I am.

I closed my eyes tighter, held my breath, and leaned into Fleming. I expected to feel the warmth from Annabeth's body flow down my arms, through my hands and into my own body. Any second, I knew there would be a flash of light, and I would wake up gasping in my own body. How shocked Fleming would be to see me sit up naked and discover he was holding the lifeless body of Annabeth.

Finally, I realized I had to either breathe or faint. I gasped for air, frustrated why my prayer had not been answered. I was getting annoyed because nothing had changed. I was still in Annabeth's body, while my own body remained lifeless. I redoubled my efforts and silently, desperately, prayed more fervently. Nothing happened. Nada. Zip. I was still in Annabeth's body. *Oh, God, what have I done to offend you?* Nothing was happening, but I couldn't give up. If I couldn't get Dad's help, then I would persuade Dr. Hopkins to help me. I leaned over and kissed my body's cheek. *Don't worry, Lindsey, we'll figure this out. I'll be back soon.*

CHAPTER SEVEN
HELL TO PAY

I slept like the dead. *Omigosh! Did I really say that?* I suspected that the night nurse put something in my IV to knock me out cold. I woke up just as my breakfast tray arrived. For some reason I was ravenous, and I cleaned my plate, even though the scrambled eggs were dry, the grits runny, the bacon half raw, and the orange juice watery. Dad always said breakfast was the most important meal of the day because it provided you energy for your daily activities.

A knock sounded on the door seconds after an orderly carried away my tray and empty plate. Before I could protest, Neeley Hill bounced into the room, crawled into my bed, and tried to hug me. Her warm Juicy Fruit-smelling breath invaded my nose. Suddenly, my stomach started cramping, my head was splitting, and the chills and fever had returned. Starting to feel downright cranky, I shoved her off the bed. "What're you doing?"

She fell backwards, landing sideways in the visitor's chair. I felt maybe a tiny bit of remorse as her eyes filled with tears.

"I'm sorry, Annabeth," she said softly. "It's just I'm so happy you're not dead, I can't help myself. They said you died in ER. Never knew anyone before who died and came back to life."

Blood rushed to my head. *Yes, that was it!* The body-swapping happened in the ER. We both died, and I was brought back to life, but in the wrong body. But if my body was dead in the morgue, what had happened to Annabeth?

"Annabeth, we really need to talk, so I hope you're feeling yourself today." Neeley's voice cracked.

Oh, okay. I felt badly for her that I wasn't Annabeth. She and Neeley were obviously best friends. Like me and Rachel. If I could just figure out how to get back in my body before it started to rot, maybe Annabeth would return from wherever she was and occupy her own body, again. It would be a win-win for everyone.

Neeley reached over and poked my leg. "Annabeth, are you listening to me? I'm scared. Word's spreading on the street. Tony's out to finish us off."

Tony would have to wait. Getting back into my body had a higher priority. When my mother died, I read that as you grieve, you pass through several stages. Grieving for my body, I figured I had worked myself through denial, sadness, and pain. I wasn't normally a rude person, but now I was getting into the angry stage of grieving. I scowled at Neeley. "Don't call me Annabeth!" I pressed the nurses' call button. "Get out."

But Neeley sat frozen in the chair, staring at me like I was a roach swimming in her breakfast cereal. Deep down I knew she was a victim just like me, but my anger consumed me. "GET OUT!" I screeched, then regretted it as an intense pain tore through the top of my head.

Neeley rose from the chair, tears streaming down her scrunched-up face. "What's happened to you, girl? You look like Annabeth, but you sure don't talk like her at all."

"Oh yeah?"

"My Annabeth has a nice South Georgia drawl. Tony calls you his sweet little Magnolia. But you talk snobby and ugly to me. I want my Annabeth back. I like her. I don't like you." Neeley paused and took a deep breath. "You're acting selfish and mean to me. You're here in this hospital room all safe and sound, while I'm out there hiding from Tony. And I'm so scared, girl." Neeley choked down a sob, did an about face, and ran out the door.

I sat there in shock. Suddenly the tears were rolling down my cheeks. I slammed my fist into my pillow. "I am not Annabeth!" I yelled. Then I whispered, "But I'm not Lindsey either."

"Then who are you?"

I turned my face away from my pillow and gasped. "Justin!"

Frowning at me, Justin stood halfway between me and the open door. His cotton-blond hair stood in peaks on top of his head. He was dressed in his usual attire—jeans and a Disney shirt.

Even though I didn't like him, I was happy to see someone I knew. "Did your dad tell you I was here?"

"Didn't have to. You're the talk of the third-floor nurses' station."

I wiped my nose. "Really? What are they saying?"

"That some crazy teenage girl thinks she's in the wrong body. That she claims to be my girlfriend Lindsey."

I hissed. Justin was so annoying. "I am not your girlfriend."

He sneered. "Because you aren't Lindsey Anderson."

I felt my anger kicking into high gear. "Oh. Yes. I. Am. And I can prove it." I could remember and recite every annoying thing he'd ever done to me.

He stepped up to the edge of my bed, his eyes narrowing. "Okay, imposter. Prove it!"

"Justin, what are you doing here?" Dr. Hopkins' loud voice sounded from the door.

His face flushing, Justin jerked around to face his dad. "I just wanted to . . ."

"I don't want to hear it." Dr. Hopkins glanced at me and back to his son. "This is inappropriate behavior, young man. Go to my office and stay there."

"Yes, sir." Justin glared back at me and whispered, "We'll finish this conversation later." Then he stomped out of the room.

I leaned back into my pillow and sighed. With people talking about me, I guess I was becoming infamous.

Dr. Hopkins walked over to my bed. "How are you feeling?" he asked with professional coolness, reaching for my wrist and taking my pulse.

I grabbed his forearm. "How do you think I'm feeling?"

"I think you're getting better." He smiled and pried my fingers loose. "The nurse said you've been walking the halls without passing out."

"I don't feel any better!" I bit my quivering lower lip and fought back tears.

His face softened. "I'm sorry. Let me apologize for my son. Did he say anything to upset you?"

I shook my head. A lump rose in my throat.

"I'm doing everything I can to get you well," he said. "You'll be healthy and drug-free in no time. Withdrawal symptoms peak one to three days after your last dose. Then symptoms will subside in about a week."

"I was completely healthy and drug-free until I woke up here. Now I feel awful."

"You'd feel much worse if we discontinued your methadone therapy." Dr. Hopkins rubbed the back of his neck. "Methadone is a long-acting opioid that is a favored treatment for heroine addiction. It acts as a painkiller, fights respiratory depression, works to keep an addict calm, and lowers blood pressure. Once your heroin withdrawal symptoms are gone, then we can slowly wean you off the methadone."

Fighting to control my emotions, I took a deep breath and made an effort to remain calm. "This has been one nightmare after another," I spoke softly. "First you tell me I'm not who I think I am. Then I find out I was nearly beat to death. Now I hear that I'm heroin-addicted and taking an opioid to control my withdrawal symptoms. Can it get any worse?"

He squeezed my arm. "Let's hope not. By the way, we've contacted Family and Children's Services. As soon as you're well enough to be discharged, they'll find you a foster home—unless, of course, you want us to call your parents or a legal guardian."

"Family and Children's Services?" But I already had a parent. Besides, I'd only heard bad things about foster kids. Didn't they carry their belongings around in plastic garbage bags? Weren't they often abused or mistreated? I couldn't let them carry me off to live with strangers.

"Who are you and why are you passing yourself off as my daughter?"

I jerked my head around to focus on the man who had quietly stepped into the room.

"Daddy!" I shrieked, overcome with joy. Everything was going to be all right now. I held out my arms to him for a hug. Dr. Epting had come through after all.

Dad backed up against the door, his face twisted in anguish.

It was like my heart was being ground into hamburger. Worse than I imagined.

Dr. Hopkins walked over to Dad. "Reggie, are you all right?"

"I can't believe you talked me into coming here, Steve" Dad said to him.

"Talk to her, Reggie. She really believes she's Lindsey."

My heart dropped. I swear I heard the thud when it hit the floor. My own dad was here at last, but it wasn't the joyous reunion I had anticipated.

Dad shook his head. "No, Steve, this is a mistake." He stepped toward the door.

"Wait! Don't go!" I yelled. "Listen to me, please! This is the weirdest thing that's ever happened to me, but I have it all figured out." Dad always loved it when I figured out something on my own. Logic and analytical skills were important to him. He had to have scientific proof and cold hard facts.

Dr. Hopkins grabbed Dad's elbow and turned him around. "Five minutes, Reggie. Consider it a second opinion or a special consultation. You can even send me a bill."

Dad sat down, but not close enough that I could touch him. He looked ill. His face was pale, and his bloodshot, swollen eyes had dark circles underneath. I hadn't seen him look this bad since Mom died. "Are you all right, Daddy?"

He turned paler and rubbed his right hand across his mouth and lower jaw. His eyes narrowed. "Why do you think you're my daughter?" he asked hoarsely, his hands tightly gripping the arms of the chair.

I could tell he had his emotions in check. He was speaking with his clinical, indifferent voice. I leaned as close to him as I could get. "Because I _am_ your daughter. I know it's hard to believe, Daddy, but this is me, your daughter, Lindsey. Ask me about anything. You'll see."

I saw a red flush creeping out from under Dad's collar. He clinched his jaw, but he didn't blink. "My daughter was hospitalized in the eighth grade . . ."

I smiled as the memory flooded back. "Yes, I had the flu and pneumonia."

I heard a strangled sound from Dad. My smile faded. "Dad?"

He jumped to his feet, wide-eyed and breathing heavily.

I had to get his attention before he ran out of the room screaming. "It was Halloween and you brought me a skull that screeched every time anyone came into my room."

"I don't believe this," Dad said, backing toward the door.

"Don't go, Daddy. Help me. I know my body is downstairs in the morgue. Surely you can figure out a way to get me back into it, can't you?"

Dad's face turned dark red and a strangled sound came from deep inside his throat. He turned and fled the room.

"Daddy!" A sob escaped my throat.

Dr. Hopkins opened and closed his mouth, but said nothing.

"Make him come back," I pleaded. "I didn't get this way on purpose."

He shook his head and followed Dad out of the room. I was overcome with feelings of impending doom. I was all alone. No one loved me. No one cared about me. For the first time that I could remember, I had no one. A lump formed in my throat. Then I glanced at the photo on the nightstand. Only one person claimed to be my friend. My best friend. And I didn't want anything to do with her. Ironic, wasn't it? I sobbed until I fell asleep from exhaustion.

CHAPTER EIGHT
SEARCHING FOR TRUTH

A shaft of light from the hallway illuminated the wall clock in my hospital room. Midnight. Bits and pieces of Dad's visit floated through my mind. It was obvious Dad wouldn't help. It was up to me. This pity party was over.

I dozed off after the crack-of-dawn nurse came through to check my pulse and blood pressure. I awakened to the smell of bacon, eggs, and coffee, and the hushed voices of two men talking just inside the door to my room. Pretending to be asleep, I eavesdropped. Mom would have been horrified. I didn't care. This was self-preservation.

Through squinted eyes, I saw a short, rotund, bearded man standing next to Dr. Epting. His hands were balled into tight fists. His jaw clenched so tightly that ligaments protruded from his neck. "Do you realize how crazy that sounds?" he asked.

"It's the opportunity of a lifetime, Albert. This could put St. Mary's on the map."

Albert? Who was he?

"We'll pass, thank you."

"One phone call and a team of parapsychologists can leave Los Angeles tonight and be running their tests here tomorrow."

Parapsychologists? What were they talking about? Were they like ghost busters?

The bearded doctor threw up his hands. "Bill, they're nothing but charlatans. This girl is suffering from amnesia."

"How does she know all those details about Lindsey?"

I held my breath. They were talking about _me_. Dr. Epting really believed that I was Lindsey. But why bring in parapsychologists? Did I look like a lab rat?

"Maybe she reads the society section."

"I doubt if she reads any newspaper," Dr. Epting said. "And even if she does, that doesn't explain how she knew Lindsey was a soccer star."

The one called Albert shrugged. "That was on the front page of the sports section. Or maybe she overheard someone talking in ER. How should I know?"

"That's just it, isn't it? You don't."

"Bill, real-life patients don't get revived in the wrong body." The bearded doctor walked over to the sink and threw some water on his face, drying it off with a paper towel. He sighed. "Okay, Bill, for argument's sake, let's say that Lindsey Anderson's soul or her entity is somehow inside Annabeth Shepard's body."

I exhaled slowly. Yes, I wanted to hear this.

Dr. Epting twisted his purple tie and smiled a lipless smile. "Yes?"

"How is this possible?"

The white-haired psychologist stood silently for a few seconds. "Well, if I had to make a guess . . ."

"Yes?"

"How's this? Both women died in the ER at approximately the same time. Annabeth from a brutal beating and Lindsey from sudden cardiac death."

Sudden cardiac death? *Holy crap!* I almost rolled off the bed. Wasn't that something that killed high school athletes? But I always passed my annual physical.

"Of course," Albert continued, "we're waiting on the autopsy to confirm that's what she died of."

"Maybe it wasn't Lindsey's time to die," Dr. Epting suggested. "Maybe her spirit was sent back. But Annabeth's body was the only one available."

A lump formed in my throat.

"So Lindsey ended up in Annabeth's body?" Albert asked. "And Annabeth ended up out of luck?"

"Yes, exactly."

"You're the one the parapsychologists should examine." Albert walked away. Dr. Epting glanced at me over his shoulder, before following him out of the room.

CHAPTER NINE
THE TRUTH HURTS

I must have fallen asleep because when I opened my eyes, Dr. Hopkins was standing at the foot of my bed. The wall clock showed that it was 4 p.m.

"Feeling better?" he asked.

"No." I glared at him. And suddenly the anger I felt earlier, returned twofold. I was angry at Dad for deserting me, angry that my body had died, and angry at Dr. Hopkins because he was here and convenient.

Sounding hurt, he asked, "Aren't I helping you with your withdrawal symptoms?"

"So? You want a gold star?"

He flinched. "I'm doing everything I can to make you feel better, young lady."

"It's not enough." I felt absolutely miserable—mentally and physically. Maybe making Dr. Hopkins miserable would make me feel better. Besides, don't they say that desperate times call for desperate measures? And at the moment, I was feeling really desperate.

"Let me tell you something that you don't know. Another doctor and I ran off the two men who were attacking you and your friend. I saved your life or you wouldn't be here today."

"That's right, if you hadn't saved Annabeth, then I wouldn't be here today. I would still be in Lindsey Anderson's body. If you really want to help, you can start believing me. Then you can figure out a way to put me back into my real body before it gets carried off to the funeral home."

Dr. Hopkins stared at me. His eyes widened.

"What would you do if Justin woke up in another person's body?"

His body jolted ever so slightly, but I sensed alarm bells going off in his head.

"Wouldn't you do everything possible to help get his body back?" I noticed beads of sweat popping out on his forehead. "You would do anything, because Justin is your son. Your only child." I was happy to see that I startled him.

"Who told you that?"

"Nobody told me that. I'm in Justin's human biology class. Remember when you visited our class? We had to prick our fingers and look at our blood under the microscope. I was the one who squealed, 'My blood's moving!' And you said, 'That's a good thing, Miss Anderson, or you would be dead.'"

"How do you know that?"

Realizing his doubts were crumbling, I sat up and glared at Dr. Hopkins. "Aren't you listening to me? <u>I am Lindsey Anderson</u>, and I'm in somebody else's body."

Dr. Hopkins collapsed in the visitor's chair. "This isn't possible."

"Why not?" The more I learned about science, the more it seemed that anything was possible. How could anyone look under a microscope at life in a drop of pond scum or through a telescope at another galaxy and not have an attitude adjustment?

Dr. Hopkins started gulping down air.

A calmness swept throughout my body. "You're hyperventilating."

"You're right," he gasped and took a deep breath.

"That's right. Slow and easy." Gradually his breathing slowed down. Color returned to his face. I began to hope that he might be willing to help me,

Elbows on his knees, Dr. Hopkins dropped his face into his hands and shook his head. "I am not having this conversation with you."

"That's what I've been telling myself for days. I do not understand what has happened to me. How would you feel if one morning you woke up in the body of a homeless guy who lives in a cardboard box and eats out of garbage cans?" I fell back against my pillow.

Dr. Hopkins lifted his head. "I don't know what to say. Nothing in my life—nothing in my medical training—has prepared me for anything like this." His eyes locked with mine. "Are you really Lindsey Anderson?"

"I'm afraid so. Will you write up my experience in a medical journal?"

"Only if you have ambitions to be a freak show star." His voice cracked, and he wiped his eyes with the back of his hand.

My heart beat faster. "Dr. Hopkins, will you please help me?" I willed myself to remain calm. Now that he realized the truth about my situation, surely he would want to do everything in his power to help me. Wasn't that part of his Hippocratic Oath?

Dr. Hopkins leaned toward me. "How could I possibly help you? How could anyone in the medical community help you? It would take a miracle to resolve this. Or a real-deal, bona fide sorcerer." He laughed. "It would take a flesh-and-blood Merlin at the very least."

Holy crap! Dr. Hopkins was losing his mind. "Stop it right there, and listen to me. I overheard some doctor called Albert talking to Dr. Epting. He said Lindsey . . . He said I died of sudden cardiac death."

Dr. Hopkins nodded. "Yes, that was Dr. McCracken. That's what we believe is the cause of Lindsey's death. It's rare, but it happens occasionally to healthy teenage athletes. Such a terrible thing." His eyes watered. "Justin is devastated."

I blinked. Why would Justin be upset? *Because he loves you, you moron! Duh!* I shook my head. I couldn't let myself get sidetracked. "Dr. Hopkins, do you have any thoughts on how to get me back in my own body? Maybe use electric shock or something?"

Dr. Hopkins clinched his jaw. "Do I look like Dr. Frankenstein?" Staring at me wide-eyed, he stood and backed toward the door.

"I'm not asking you to dig up bodies and sew body parts together." It was then that I noticed his color didn't look so good. "Dr. Hopkins, we need to do something before it's too late."

Dr. Hopkins opened the door. "It's already too late. Lindsey's body is scheduled for an autopsy tomorrow morning." Then he was out the door and gone.

I was still sitting in shock when the smiling volunteer pushed her media cart into my room. "How are you feeling today?" she chirped. "Would you be interested in any magazines or books or a copy of the Atlanta newspaper?"

Ready to shout "no," I reconsidered. "The newspaper, please." I literally snatched it from her hand. Before she could push the media cart out the door, I had opened the folded paper and smoothed out page one on the bed. Immediately, a single headline running across the bottom of the page jumped out at me: **High school soccer star dies at end of state championship game**.

I steeled myself and read the entire news story:

An 18-year-old East Lake High School senior and athlete died unexpectedly Saturday night at Atlanta's Talmage-Mitchell Stadium.

Lindsey Anderson collapsed on the soccer field after kicking the winning goal for the Girls Soccer State Championship Game between the East Lake Bombers and the Excaliburs. Anderson was pronounced dead at St. Mary's Hospital. Cause of death is currently unknown, pending results of an autopsy to be performed by Fulton County Medical Examiner's office.

"The East Lake Bombers defeated the Excaliburs 2-1 because of Miss Anderson's winning kick," according to East Lake Coach Ernest Burdine. "Everyone loved Lindsey. We are devastated by her death."

Anderson, the daughter of Dr. Richard Anderson, director of the Bosch Research Institute in Atlanta, recently received a full athletic scholarship to Stanford University and was accepted into the U.S. Youth Soccer Olympic Development Program. She was scheduled to graduate with honors from East Lake High School in two weeks.

High school counselors and grief counselors are available for staff and students. A crisis intervention team is also being made available to help students, parents, and staff.

Principal Gerald Baker said a group of students is working to organize a tribute to honor Anderson's life. "Lindsey was quite popular with our faculty, staff, and students. I don't think you could find a kid at school who would say a bad thing about her."

Loche-Schmidt Funeral Home is in charge of arrangements.

I wiped tears from my cheeks. Reading the news article made my death sound quite terminal. An autopsy? They were going to cut me open and remove my heart and liver and kidneys and examine them like on TV? Would they saw the top off my skull and examine my brain, too? Any idea of getting back my own body was quickly getting flushed down the toilet. I grabbed a tissue, blew my nose, and quickly went through the rest of the newspaper, searching for a news article on Annabeth.

Finally, on page 12, a small article under Police Blotter caught my eye: **Two doctors save lives of teenage girls**. It was only a few paragraphs, but provided some information:

Two Atlanta doctors, jogging late Saturday night in the Piedmont Park area, saved two teenage girls being attacked by two men.

Around 10 p.m., Drs. Steve Hopkins and Albert McCracken, both physicians at St. Mary's Hospital, heard women screaming in a wooded area off Charles Allen Drive and found two men attacking the teenagers. While McCracken chased away the suspects, Hopkins called 911 and performed CPR on one of the victims until EMTs arrived.

One severely beaten victim is recovering at St. Mary's Hospital. The second victim was treated and released. Since the victims are underage minors, their names have not been released.

Based on descriptions provided by the two "good Samaritans" at the scene, police believe one of the suspects could be a known drug dealer and sex trafficker operating in the area.

•   •   •   •   •   •

After my dinner tray was taken away, I washed Annabeth's face, brushed her teeth, and made an attempt to comb her stringy, blonde hair. I looked in the mirror and grimaced at the image looking back at me. It made me more determined than ever to get my body back. It seemed hopeless. Time was against me, and lack of a modern-day Frankenstein wasn't helping. Not even one magic wand. I was so screwed. But I couldn't give up. I decided to pay another visit to the hospital morgue. Maybe I could steal my body and hide it before it was taken away to be autopsied.

The nurses' station was bustling. When I told a nurse sitting behind the desk that I wanted to stretch my legs and walk some, she seemed agreeable. I tied the sad, pathetic, hospital robe around me, slipped my feet into my slippers, grabbed my IV-tree, headed to the elevator, and pressed the DOWN button.

The basement didn't look so scary this trip. I passed through the frosted glass sliding doors of the hospital morgue and rang the buzzer. My only concern was that Fleming Moore might not be on duty tonight, and I would have a lot of explaining to do. I could always say I was looking for the restroom and got lost. But I didn't have to do that. Fleming opened the door. He was surprised, yet I think he was happy to see me, too. He motioned me through the door and locked it behind me.

"What are you doing here?" he asked.

I smiled. "I wanted to check on my friend in 3127, Lindsey Anderson? Can you tell me when she is supposed to be picked up for her autopsy?"

Fleming's eyebrows went up in surprise. "How did you know about that?"

"I read it in the newspaper this morning. You would be surprised how much information you can find in a newspaper. Sometimes, it's better than Google." I stepped over to his computer.

He looked at me oddly, but sat down and began tapping on the keyboard until something appeared on his screen. He scrolled down and stopped to read. Then he turned to me and pointed at my name. "It says your friend's body was taken to the medical examiner's office about an hour before I came on duty. It's scheduled for autopsy early in the morning."

I felt the blood drain from my face down into my toes. I must have swayed or something, because Fleming helped me sit down in his chair.

"Are you all right?" he asked, looking very concerned. He was probably worried how he would explain an unconscious girl lying on the floor to his superiors. It definitely wouldn't look good for him.

He stepped over to the sink and filled a paper cup with water, and wet a paper towel. I drank the water and wiped my face with the cold, damp paper towel. It seemed to revive me. I felt less woozy. "What happens after the autopsy?" I asked softly.

Fleming checked his computer. "According to my records, Loche-Schmidt Funeral Home will pick up the remains."

I nodded. I knew what I had to do next.

CHAPTER TEN
NO TURNING BACK

After a crack-of-dawn hospital breakfast, I waited patiently until 9 o'clock. Surely any reputable funeral home would be open by then. What with dozens of folks dying to get in, right? I had already called 411 for their phone number. I punched in the numbers and listened as the phone rang four times.

The line clicked, and I heard a woman's voice. "Good morning! Loche-Schmidt Funeral Home. How may I direct your call?"

"Yes, good morning," I answered, trying not to sound like a teenage girl. "I read in the newspaper that Loche-Schmidt was in charge of arrangements for Lindsey Anderson."

"Yes, that is correct."

"Good. Could you please tell me what time is the viewing and visitation?" I don't know what I was thinking. I didn't even have a plan. I only knew I needed to be there for me. No matter what.

"I'm sorry, but there will not be a viewing. Only a private graveside and interment service Wednesday afternoon. A memorial service will take place at a later date."

My head swirled. "An interment service?"

The voice on the other end of the phone hesitated and sighed. "Yes, an interment of ashes. The body is being cremated."

Holy crap! My real body was going up in flames? I felt like someone had whammed both their fists into my stomach. As I struggled to breathe, shock waves vibrated throughout my body. It was like the day Dad picked me up at school and told me Mom was dead. But if I could live through that, I could live through this.

What was I going to do? The thought of being stuck in Annabeth's corpse for the rest of my life didn't sit well with me. What were my other options? Could I live my old life in Annabeth's body? Would that be physically possible? This body was a minus 10 on any athletic check list. No way could it pass the President's National Fitness Test. It was worn-out and drug-abused. This body was a reject even for a desperate person. *Holy crap!* I really was a desperate person.

And what about this Tony person who wanted to see this crappy body dead and buried? And Dad wanted nothing to do with me. Nobody cared about me. I wiped my eyes with the back of my hand. Just when I thought life couldn't get any worse, it did.

Suddenly, my shoulders started shaking and I sobbed loudly. I bawled uncontrollably for a good ten minutes. I was not normally such an emotional train wreck. Finally, I sat up and blew my nose. This self-pity party had gone on long enough. I needed to take control and make a plan for the rest of my life.

"Hello?"

I jerked my head around. Neeley stood, gripping the door handle. Today she wore tight red leggings that showed every bump and crevice in her crotch. In the middle of her midriff bulge protruded a pierced "outie" navel. For two seconds, my shocked fashion sensibility drowned out my despair.

"Are you all right?" Neeley's large dark brown eyes were full of concern.

I wiped my eyes and blew my nose with another hospital-issue tissue. "No, I'm not."

She entered the room cautiously. This time she did not leap on my bed or try to hug me. Instead, she stopped several feet away. "The doctor said I shouldn't upset you."

"That's right, don't upset me." Even though the mere sight of her upset me, I didn't say it. No, it was in my best interest not to be rude to my new BFF. After all, at the moment, she was my only friend.

"Girlfriend, you been crying?" She slid one foot toward me.

I wiped my nose. She really sounded like she cared. I felt a little bit guilty, since I had not been very nice to her. "I heard some really bad news."

She stepped closer to the bed. "You need to get strong. We gotta leave town ASAP. Time's running out. How can I help? You need me to get you some stuff?"

"Stuff?" What was she talking about?

"A little crack, maybe?" She edged closer.

I couldn't believe it. Here I was, suffering from Annabeth's addiction and Neeley wanted to get me more drugs. Some best friend. "Thank you, but I don't need any stuff."

"Aren't your insides turning wrong-side out? I seen you shaking. You know you gotta have something. Then you can get outta that bed."

I wanted to get out of this bed, too, but not to head off into the sunset with her.

One final step and Neeley was next to my bed. The acrid smell of stale sweat intermingled with Juicy Fruit and some kind of cheap floral-citrus cologne clogged my throat. Didn't she ever take a bath? Not that I didn't need one myself. My eyes watered. Her short pudgy fingers reached toward me.

"Don't!" It would totally creep me out if she touched me.

"Annabeth, don't be mean to me!" Her chin trembled, as she pushed out her lower lip in a pout.

What are you doing, Lindsey? She believes you're her best friend Annabeth, and you need her help. Who else is there? I sighed. "Uh—I'm sorry, Neeley, my memory is—uh—fuzzy. Tell me again how you know Annabeth—uh—me?"

"Girlfriend, we are sex slaves for Tony. We've been sharing a room ever since you arrived here from Ludowici last year. Can't you remember? Your stepdad abused you, so you ran away from home. Then Tony found you begging in Piedmont Park and took you in, remember? Me and you—best friends?"

That was more information than I wanted. I inhaled a deep breath. *Come on, Lindsey, if you want your old life back, you need to stay calm and cool.* "Tell me about Tony."

Neeley clapped her hands and sat down on my bed. "Tony beat you up. And more than once."

"He beat me up before?"

"Yeah, the day you told him you was knocked up, remember?"

Pregnant? *"Holy crap!"*

"After he knocked you around, he give you money to take care of it. You gave the money to Shark for abortion pills, remember?"

My stomach started to hurt. I didn't want to hear any more, but I had to know everything I could about Annabeth. And about this body I was trapped in. "Who's Shark?"

"Shark? Don't you remember nothing? Everybody knows Shark. He works here at St. Mary's. You get shot, he gets you fixed up, no questions. You need abortion pills, he gets 'em for you—for a price."

Obviously, a nice guy. A team player. Someone I didn't want to know. Someone who works in this hospital? I shivered at the thought. Did he know I was here? Was he waiting for the right moment to come in and cut my throat? Goose bumps broke out on my arms. "And Tony's money?"

"You stole it, so we could get away from Tony." Neeley was so excited, her whole body jiggled and wiggled all over.

"You really don't have it?" I crossed my fingers, hoping she had the money stuffed away somewhere.

"Not me, girlfriend. You hid it where they can't find it." She looked at me expectantly like I was going to pull the money out of my hospital gown and hand it to her.

I shook my head. "What money are you talking about?"

Neeley looked at me with total disbelief. "Girlfriend, we're talking about all of Tony's money—the money us girls make, his drug money, his protection money—even Angelo's cut." She lowered her voice to a near whisper. "And if Angelo don't get his share, then Tony's dead meat."

My splitting headache returned. I frowned. I really didn't like where this story was going. No wonder Tony tried to kill Annabeth. He must have been desperate. "Are we talking about a lot of money?"

"Whoo-ee, girl!" She pointed a finger at me. "That bag was stuffed full of twenties, fifties, and hundred-dollar bills.

Thousands and thousands of dollars. And a black notebook filled with names, numbers, and dates. We thought we done died and gone to heaven. You said we was gonna move far away—like Seattle or San Francisco. That we was gonna get our GEDs and take some classes at a technical school. You said I could maybe get a job as an office receptionist, if I learned word processing. You said you was gonna become a nurse."

I fought down a feeling of nausea. "I stole this money knowing Tony would kill me to get it back?"

"Uh-huh."

"That's crazy!"

"Like I didn't tell you that myself." Neeley glanced at the door. "Damn, girl, you didn't have time to think about it. While Tony was slapping you around, the key to the money locker just fell into your hands and he didn't see a thing," she said in a hushed voice. "I thought taking the money was a lousy idea at first, but the more I think about getting away from here and starting a new life, the better I feel about it." She reached back behind herself and tugged on the seam of her tight pants that was riding in her crack.

A chill rippled down my spine at the thought of being chased and killed. Neeley bounced on my bed, but I didn't complain. "I don't understand. If Tony was so mean to us, why didn't we just leave?"

Neeley covered her mouth with both hands and laughed. "And go where? If we stayed in Atlanta, Tony would get us sooner or later. We're his property, don't you know? He say he has money invested in us. Anyway, with no money, we couldn't leave town. Don't you see?"

No, not really, but the picture was getting clearer. It didn't sound like Annabeth could call her mother and return home. I felt a lump in my throat. Calling home certainly hadn't worked for me. We sat in silence for a minute or two. I reached over and touched Neeley's hand. "I'm sorry things have been so bad for you."

"For you, too, girlfriend." She looked at me with her big, dark-brown eyes. "You know, Annabeth, it was all my fault Tony found us."

I pulled my hand away from hers. "What do you mean?"

"Remember how we was hiding in that hole of a hotel?"

"Remind me."

"Well, you got to feeling bad and needed some 'stuff' to make you feel better."

"You mean drugs?"

"Yeah." She twisted a curl round and round her pudgy finger and lowered her voice to a whisper. "I tried to get you some 'stuff' from Dixie. How was I to know that Dante was hiding at her place."

"Dante?" With a name like that he had to be a bad person.

"Uh-huh. Dante is Tony's protector, and he does bad stuff to anybody Tony don't like. He called Tony and followed me back to the hotel."

I cringed at the sheer horror of her story. Bad things happened at school—bullying and beatings, stolen laptops and cell phones, date rape—but nothing that could compare with this. "Are you saying they broke into our hotel room and beat me?" My voice came out strangled.

"Oh, no, they waited until we left to pick up the money Saturday night and take the next bus out of town." She sat up on the side of the bed.

I let out a long breath that I didn't realize I had been holding. "What happened?" It came out a strangled whisper.

"When you saw them following us, we started running through Piedmont Park. But they grabbed us and dragged us into the woods. Dante held me down, while Tony worked you over good. He wanted to know where his money was, but you wouldn't tell him. He kept hitting you and kicking you and you never said a word." Neeley patted my arm. "You were so brave."

Brave? Actually it sounded pretty stupid to me. But being a sex slave sounded really bad. I could not imagine just how bad. In Annabeth's situation, I probably would have been desperate enough to steal his money bag, too.

Neeley swallowed and took a deep breath. "Then these two white guys—the doctors here—heard us screaming and came running to rescue us."

This was more than I could handle. I closed my eyes tightly. My eyes burned as they filled with tears. I was Lindsey Anderson, high school soccer star. In the fall, I was going to Stanford on a full, athletic scholarship. I might be stuck in Annabeth's pathetic body, but I would rather die than live Annabeth's sad, broken life.

CHAPTER ELEVEN
OUT OF THE FRYING PAN

An intimidating physical therapist—introducing himself as Mike the motivator—ran Neeley out of my room. When I looked up at this really tall, good-looking young man with shoulder-length blond hair, my jaw dropped. He reminded me of some of the men on the covers of Harlequin romance novels. Not that I ever read any. He had to be 6 feet 5 inches tall and, like my soccer coach, not someone who'd take "no" for an answer. So when he said we were going for a walk, I didn't argue.

Mike helped me into a flimsy hospital robe and hoisted me to my feet. Gripping the IV-tree for support, and with Mike's firm hand on my shoulder, I stumbled toward the door. Mike led me down the long hallway and into areas of the hospital I had not seen before. Even though I felt much stronger than yesterday when I visited the morgue, I knew I would tire if he kept nudging me along at such a fast pace. Soon we were in an area without patient rooms or nurses' stations. A quiet area without anyone else around. Alarm bells began ringing in my head.

"Uh, Mike? I'm getting sort of tired. I want to go back to my room." I stopped and looked up into his eyes.

"Okay, kid, this works for me." Then he grabbed my throat with both hands and began to squeeze. I couldn't breathe. I grabbed his hands, but they were like an iron vise. Just as my eyes were bulging out of their sockets, I yanked up my knee and hammered him in his manly parts like they were a soccer ball.

The second he grunted, cursed, and released his hold on my neck, I let out a bloodcurdling scream and ran, yanking out the IV that tethered me to the pole. With blood spurting out of my arm, I continued running and screaming. I could hear what sounded like a charging bull behind me, but I didn't look back. His ragged breathing alerted me that he was closing in, but I rounded the next corner and fell into the arms of two hospital guards. Mike disappeared through the staircase doors.

The guards chaperoned me back to my room. I knew I was in trouble. At least Annabeth's body was in serious trouble, and since I was now in possession of her body, that meant me, too. Goose bumps broke out on my arms. *Holy crap!* I almost died, again! I needed to get out of this hospital. I suddenly started remembering all the TV shows I'd seen in which hospital patients were murdered. Smothered to death. Or lethal stuff shot into their IVs. Or worse.

By the time the nurses and Dr. Hopkins carefully examined me, the doctor I had seen earlier talking with Dr. Epting walked through the door. He nodded to Dr. Hopkins. "The police have been notified. They'll be here soon."

As if that were a secret signal, the nurses left.

"Annabeth, this is Dr. Albert McCracken. He was with me the day that drug dealer tried to kill you."

Dr. McCracken smiled through his mustache and beard, and extended his hands to grasp mine. They were large hands, but they felt warm and comforting to me. "Speaking for St. Mary's, I want to tell you how sorry we are about what happened to you."

He squeezed my hands tightly before releasing them. I smiled back at him. Somehow Dr. McCracken made me feel safe.

"What just happened to you needs to be taken seriously," Dr. Hopkins said, arms crossed.

"Your life is in great danger. You need to leave the hospital and go somewhere safe. Some place where you can continue to receive excellent medical care," Dr. McCracken said, tugging on his beard.

The doctors looked worried, and they were echoing what Neeley kept telling me. I didn't like that. Did they know about Tony and the stolen money? "Couldn't you just put a policeman outside my door to guard me?"

Dr. Hopkins and Dr. McCracken pulled chairs over and sat down. "We could," explained Dr. Hopkins, "but it would be safer and better for you and St. Mary's if we move you out of the hospital."

"Detective Richards' solution is to have a policeman outside your door." Dr. McCracken's voice was soft and soothing. "However, that might frighten our patients and visitors, and could possibly place everyone in danger. Dr. Hopkins and I believe getting you to a safe place is a better choice."

I raised a brow questioningly. He sounded like Dad trying to get me to do something I didn't want to do. But at the moment, I had my own game plan. I was leaving the hospital, all right, but not to be babysat at some safe house. I was going to see Dad. Once I convinced him I really was his daughter, he'd let me move back home. He would protect me from Tony. I could be Lindsey

Anderson, again. I would just look a little bit different. Actually, a whole lot different, but at least I'd be breathing.

"Besides someone trying to kill you, we also have to deal with parapsychologists flying in from Los Angeles." Dr. McCracken said.

"Dr. Epting's ghostbusters?" I asked.

Dr. McCracken sighed and pinched at his mustache. "Parapsychologists research and investigate all types of paranormal phenomena, like poltergeists . . ."

I turned my attention back to the doctor. "UFOs ?" I suggested.

"Psychic abilities, ESP, telepathy . . ." continued Dr. McCracken.

I twitched my nose. "Body switching."

Dr. McCracken nodded and sighed heavily. "Yes, all of the above. The members in this particular group are known for being very intense and thorough."

"They're crack pots," said Dr. Hopkins.

"They want to study you. Analyze you. Dissect you." Dr. McCracken said bluntly.

I groaned inwardly. Imagine that. They want to analyze an 18-year-old high school student stuck in a 14-year-old hooker's body? Would that be considered a scientific phenomenon for someone in the parapsychological arena? I pictured my photo on the cover of every tabloid in the country. I could see the headlines: **High school soccer star wakes up in teen hooker's body**. I'd become infamous. And that would end any hopes of ever connecting with Dad. He hated the tabloids and all the "freaky" stories in them. I sighed and felt the fight drain out of me.

"This could evolve into a media circus," Dr. Hopkins pointed out. "Or worse, we could attract the unwanted attention of certain unnamed government agencies."

Yeah, I could become an X-File or a Roswell alien and just disappear. No one would ever know what happened to me. And not a single person would notice my absence or even care. I gulped and swallowed hard. Certainly not my dad. As far as he was concerned, I was already dead, cremated, interred, and gone.

"The police are concerned about your safety," Dr. Hopkins said. "They don't know if the man who nearly killed you today is out there waiting for another chance. They want you to testify in court against the men who attacked you and your friend in Piedmont Park. Your testimony could help them take down large sex trafficking and drug rings."

How could I testify against anyone who attacked Annabeth on the same night that I was dying on the soccer field? But I guess they would figure that out eventually. I wish I knew what Tony and Dante looked like. At least that way I'd recognize them, if I saw them coming.

Dr. McCracken moved to the side of my bed and sat down, taking my hands into his. "Now do you understand why it's important to leave the hospital?"

I nodded. It was a no-brainer. Unless I wanted to star in my own freak show or evaporate into thin air or be murdered, I had to leave St. Mary's. But once I left the hospital, would I really be safer?

A knock sounded on the door. Lt. Richards peeked in. "Is it safe? That pushy nurse isn't in here, is she?"

"No," said Dr. Hopkins. "The coast is clear."

"You're just in time," Dr. McCracken said, shaking the detective's hand. "We explained to Annabeth how we are taking her to a safe house before another attempt is made on her life. We don't want to endanger her life or the lives of our other patients and staff."

"What about Family and Children's Services, detective?" Dr. Hopkins asked. "Were you able to smooth everything over with them?"

"Yes, not a problem. As long as she is in protective custody, they are satisfied for the moment." Lt. Richards stood at the foot of my bed, rolling and unrolling the brim of his worn fedora hat, and staring at me. "Two attempts have been made on your life. Are you able to identify any of the perps?"

Realizing I needed to play a role for the benefit of the detective, I jumped right in. "I definitely could identify the man who choked me here in the hospital, but I still don't remember anything else. However, Neeley Hill can certainly identify the men who attacked us." I tried to provide enough information to satisfy the detective without revealing anything that might get this body arrested. Was it against the law to steal a drug dealer's money?

Lt. Richards scribbled something on his notepad. "Do you know why he tried to kill you?"

I shrugged. "That part is still hazy. Neeley thinks he heard we were planning to leave town."

Lt. Richards grunted. "Were you?"

I rubbed at the tattoo on my finger. "Maybe."

"Or maybe you were holding back money to purchase drugs or something?"

I met his eyes straight on. "I honestly don't remember. Anything is possible." I bit my lower lip. All this talk about Tony scared me. Not only did I have to worry about any laws Annabeth might have broken that could send me to prison, but somewhere out there was this dangerous man who wanted me dead.

"It would help if we knew why he wants to kill you," said Lt. Richards. "Sounds personal. I don't like it. But we've issued arrest warrants for Tony and Dante for attempted murder, sex trafficking, and drug dealing, to name a few. Getting those two off the streets will be good." Lt. Richards pulled two photographs out of his inside jacket pocket and held them up in front of me. "Do either of these men look familiar to you? Any alarm bells sounding?"

I stared long and hard at both photos. One man had a thin, pale face with narrowed eyes and long, copper-colored dreadlocks. He looked angry and dangerous. The second man had a dark complexion, a thick neck, muscular shoulders, and a bald head. But what caught my attention was the earring in his left ear—a skull and crossbones. I shuddered and shook my head. "No, I don't remember ever seeing either one of them."

"Will Annabeth's testimony be crucial for a conviction?" asked Dr. Hopkins, nodding in my direction.

I turned ice cold with fear. I had no memories of Annabeth's life. If a conviction depended on my testimony, then Tony would never go to jail.

"If her memory doesn't return, then it will be up to you two and Miss Hill to testify in court," Lt. Richards said. "Are you sure her amnesia is permanent?"

My pulse quickened. I knew it was, but what would he say?

Dr. McCracken squeezed my hand. "Yes, detective, we're absolutely sure."

"Not that it matters," pointed out Lt. Richards. "As long as Tony doesn't know that she doesn't know or doesn't believe she doesn't know, she'll remain at the top of his 'hit' list."

All three men stared directly at me.

Holy crap! I was so totally screwed!

•　　•　　•　　•　　•

The door to my room opened around midnight. A shaft of light from the hallway cut across the floor toward my bed. I expected the chirpy, blonde night nurse to come in and check my vitals. Instead, Dr. McCracken entered, pushing a wheelchair.

I sat up in bed. "What are you doing?"

He parked the wheelchair next to the bed and grabbed my hospital robe off the chair. "Are you ready to go?"

"Now?" I asked, slipping into the thin cotton robe. "Isn't it a little late for joyriding up and down the hallways?"

"Shhh," he hissed, glancing over his shoulder at the partially open door. "We don't want anyone to know that you're leaving the hospital."

"Yes, but where am I going?" I had agreed to leave the hospital, but no one said where I would be going. I wanted to go someplace safe, but not to a home for the mentally ill.

"Sit down!" he whispered.

Realizing there was no sense arguing—even his whisper reeked of authority, just like Dad's—I stepped into my hospital slippers, tied my robe, and sat down in the wheelchair.

Dr. McCracken parked me at the door long enough to grab a burgundy backpack out of the closet and drop it on my lap. "Don't forget your personal effects."

"That isn't mine!" I had never seen it before. My own book bag was soft Italian leather with thick shoulder pads. I hadn't carried a canvas backpack since fifth grade.

"It belongs to the body you're inhabiting. Perhaps something inside the bag will help us understand what's going on." He looked cautiously up and down the hallway and headed left toward the elevators.

I clutched the backpack and ran my hands over the worn canvas. Maybe Dr. McCracken was right. Maybe I could find a clue in the bag about the stolen money. If I returned the money to Tony, would all be forgiven? Or would he kill me no matter what?

We paused in front of the elevators, and Dr. McCracken pressed the DOWN button. A hospital orderly stood nearby, leaning on a cart loaded down with a mop, bucket, and cleaning supplies. He wore a blue jumpsuit with the St. Mary's logo embroidered on the shirt pocket. His complexion was so dark, the whites of his eyes popped out like a cat's eyes in the dark. His shaved head shone in the overhead lights, as he watched us through hooded black eyes. I couldn't help but think of the snake that tried to kill Harry Potter.

Turning his back to us, the orderly pulled a cell phone from his pants pocket and flipped it open. The elevator doors opened, and Dr. McCracken pushed me in.

The orderly's whispery voice carried into the elevator as the doors closed, "She's checkin' out."

Was the orderly talking about me? Was he Shark, on his way to my room to recover the missing money? "Dr. McCracken, do you know that man?"

Dr. McCracken pressed the basement button. "Sure. He's worked here for years. Why?"

"He seemed awfully interested in us."

"He's always interested in everybody and everything. Shark's just that kind of guy."

I shivered. "Neeley Hill said Tony has an inside man at St. Mary's who sells him drugs. His name is Shark, too"

Dr. McCracken shook his head. "That couldn't be this Shark. He was Employee of the Year two years in a row. Nice family man."

Yeah, nice family man, but what are the odds that two men named Shark are both working at St. Mary's?

When the elevator doors opened in the basement, it was eerily quiet. The corridor was lined with unused beds, wheelchairs, and carts. I didn't like it. "What are we doing down here? Why can't we go out the main entrance?"

"We're sneaking you out in the middle of the night, and you want to go out the front door?"

He cut a corner too quickly and nearly ran down two young nurses. Not bothering to slow down, he yelled out an apology over his right shoulder. "Sorry, but we're in a hurry."

"Not so fast, please," I said, looking over my shoulder to see if Shark had followed us. "If I die, again, there might not be a spare body available."

He slowed his pushing pace. "I'd save the jokes for later. You may need them."

Pausing in front of a heavy metal door marked "Exit," Dr. McCracken pushed it open with his hip, pulling me and the wheelchair out backwards. A late model Oldsmobile idled in the alleyway outside the door. A pale-faced Dr. Hopkins stood on the sidewalk with something in his arms. I strained to see what it was and gasped. It was Neeley, her face covered in blood.

CHAPTER TWELVE
TROUBLE ARRIVES

Neeley opened her eyes and reached out to me. "Annabeth . . ."

Her face was so bloody and swollen, I hardly recognized her. Tony did this. There was not a doubt in mind. I sat frozen in the wheelchair, unable to move or speak. Then suddenly I remembered my mother's favorite horror movie: *My Blood Runs Cold*. Because now I understood what that meant.

Dr. McCracken gently eased Neeley down to the concrete sidewalk and knelt beside her. "Don't try to talk," he said. With a shaking hand, he wiped Neeley's face with his handkerchief. "Steve, get out of here—*now*. I'll take this girl to ER."

Neeley grabbed Dr. McCracken's wrist and lifted her head. "Tony's coming . . . he wants his money . . . save Annabeth." She closed her eyes, her head fell sideways.

Holy crap! Was she dead? I wished I had been nicer to her. "Neeley?" I reached down to her, but Dr. Hopkins pulled me out of the wheelchair and hauled me to the car. "Is she alive?" I asked, as he opened the passenger door and helped me inside.

"She's still breathing," Dr. McCracken said. "Somebody did a number on her, but she'll be all right."

Not "somebody"—Tony. Goosebumps broke out on my arms, and the hair on the back of my head stood up. Neeley was in bad shape, and I was next. Would I be any safer outside the hospital?

Dr. McCracken lifted Neeley off the concrete and into the wheelchair. "Go, Steve. Looks like you really will need Lt. Richards' around-the-clock security."

By the time Dr. Hopkins opened the driver's door and slid behind the steering wheel, my teeth were chattering.

"Cold?" he asked, slipping off his white medical coat and draping it across me. "Those hospital robes are thin."

"I'm not cold," I said. "I'm scared."

"So am I." Dr. Hopkins released the brake and drove down the alley between the main hospital building and the parking deck.

As we passed the parking deck, I saw an old, gray Buick stopped inside the employee exit. The light from a nearby lamp post illuminated the driver's dark face and bald head. *Shark?*

I tried to turn in my seat to see if the Buick would follow, but I couldn't get a good look. Just as I opened my mouth to mention what I saw, Dr. Hopkins' cell phone rang.

He fumbled it out of his pocket and glanced at the caller ID and then at me. "It's your friend Dr. Epting." He touched the phone and held it to his ear. "Yes?" he said with annoyance. "Bill, now is not a good time. Is there a problem?" He glanced at me. "Yes, I know Miss Shepard left the hospital. Uh-huh. What can I say, Bill? I guess she didn't like how she was being treated. How should I know where she lives? Somewhere off Metropolitan Parkway most likely. You could always ask around the neighborhood, but I wouldn't recommend it."

After Dr. Hopkins put away his phone, we drove in silence. I didn't mention my suspicions about Shark. It seemed crazy after thinking about it. Neeley's run-in with Tony had me rattled. I tried to focus my thoughts on Dad and my best friend Rachel. If there was any hope of me getting my life back, somehow I had to convince the two of them I was still alive. Dad always said it's what's inside that counts. He just didn't want to believe I was inside Annabeth.

Deep down, I knew Annabeth would never look exactly like Lindsey. But I could make it work. Maybe I could talk Dad into paying for a few physical enhancements. Like dyeing Annabeth's mousy-blah hair auburn red. Maybe some blue-tinted contacts. Then a little plastic surgery. With a good trainer, I could gain a few pounds and get this body into shape. I would have the whole summer to turn this puny body into a soccer star. Annabeth was on the petite side, but her legs were long and that might be an asset.

In the fall, if all went well, I could begin my new life at Stanford. Who there would know what Lindsey Anderson looked like anyway? And everyone else—who knew me as I used to look—would eventually adjust to the new me. People were always stealing other people's identities. Any recruiters who saw me on the field probably wouldn't remember what I looked like anyway. Of course, this would only work as long as Stanford didn't find out my old body died. What were the odds they heard it on the news? We could tell them it was a misunderstanding. A mistaken identity.

Dr. Hopkins slowed the car, turned into a driveway, and stopped. "This is it," he said, turning off the ignition.

These were the first words he'd spoken since leaving the hospital. I guess we both had plenty to think about.

When we turned off the main road, I recognized the subdivision—an old established neighborhood in North Atlanta. Dr. Hopkins stopped the car in front of a wheat-colored-brick house with dark brown shutters. Every room in the house was lighted, and the front porchlight illuminated several large oak trees in the front yard and a flower garden full of pansies beneath the front windows.

"Who lives here?" I asked.

"I do—with my wife and son."

It was hard to imagine Justin with a mother. Would Justin spend the evening vilifying me? Was it too much to hope that he was visiting his grandparents? I wasn't sure if I would be able to play nice with him or he with me.

I grabbed Dr. Hopkins' hands and eased myself out of the car. I could not believe how my run-in with Mike the Motivator had left me sore and weak. Still, I could say that I was stronger now than I had been Sunday. Two days ago, I couldn't have done this. All that hall walking and running away from a murderer had built up my strength. Any day now, I would be kicking that soccer ball around.

Once inside Dr. Hopkins' home, I sat down on a brown and gold-striped sofa by the door and dropped the backpack. A heavy oak coffee table covered with professional medical journals and news magazines was next to the sofa. Tennis trophies and framed photographs lined the top of the fireplace mantle. The room had a warm, welcoming family feel about it. I felt myself relax.

"How are you doing?" Dr. Hopkins asked, sitting beside me.

"I've felt better." I leaned back against the back of the sofa. I knew I felt a whole lot better than Neeley. I shivered. I promised myself that I owed Neeley big time. That I would make sure there would be money to get her away from Tony, so she could start her life over.

"Are you still cold?" He grabbed a throw from the end of the sofa and draped it around me. "Your body's been through a lot. I'm sorry we had to move you, but we're only trying to keep you safe."

"I know, and I appreciate that. But I'm worried about Neeley." Actually, I was feeling pretty guilty about how I had treated her. She had been beaten, and it was my fault. I should have taken her more seriously. And been nicer to her. My throat tightened.

Dr. Hopkins rose to his feet. "I'll call Dr. McCracken and see how she's doing. In the meantime, why don't I get you something to eat or drink."

"A Cherry Coke?" I could already taste the fruity sweetness.

He nodded. "I heard from the nurses that that seemed to be your drink of choice."

"That would be good." I tried to smile. "Thank you."

After he left the room, I pulled Annabeth's backpack onto my lap and unzipped the main compartment. Eew! It smelled like my gym locker—a mixture of stale sweat, mold, and mildew. I reached inside and removed a fistful of clothes.

Yuck! With two fingers, I held up a bright-orange, ultra-short, skimpy dress with spaghetti straps. Tossing it to the floor, I dug down further and pulled out a pair of deep-purple pumps with 6-inch stiletto heels and a pair of well-worn tennis shoes. Under the shoes, carefully folded, I found two more near-nothing dresses, a pair of zebra-print leggings, two micro-mini-skirts, a long-sleeve denim shirt, and several tank tops.

I grunted at the apparent absence of underwear. Not even a nice thong. Dumping the remaining items onto the cocktail table,

I found a hairbrush, toiletries, make-up, a small blue notebook, and a string of red glass beads. In a side zippered compartment was a MARTA card, some change, and a small bronze key with a blue-plastic cap.

I turned the key over in my hand. The number 252 was printed in white letters on the cap. How curious! Maybe Neeley was right. Maybe Annabeth had hidden the money and maybe this key was the clue to where it was. When I saw Dr. Hopkins returning with two steaming mugs, I tucked the key back into the small outside pocket and zipped it close.

He grinned sheepishly and offered me a mug. "Sorry, but we're out of Cokes. I made some tea and sweetened it with a spoonful of honey. That's the way Bridget—my wife—fixes it."

Holding the steaming mug with both hands, I took a sip. Cherry Coke would have been better, but tea was okay. "Thank you."

"You're welcome."

"Did you reach Dr. McCracken?" Please say Neeley's going to be okay. *Please, please, please.*

"She's in ICU with a concussion and a broken nose, but she'll be all right."

I felt the tension release from my body. "Thanks for letting me know."

He nodded. "How about something to eat? Soup, maybe? I'm really good with a can opener."

My stomach felt a little bit queasy, but maybe a little bit of soup would help. "Do you have chicken noodle?"

"I believe so." He sat down on the sofa beside me. "What's this?" he asked, reaching for the notebook.

But I was faster and snatched it out of his reach. "That's not yours."

"If you're not Annabeth, then it isn't yours either."

"Dr. McCracken said the backpack belongs to this body. Anyway, possession is nine-tenths of the law." I jutted out my lower lip into a pout.

Dr. Hopkins laughed. "Fine, keep it." He stood and walked to the window, peeking through the drapes. "I see the police have arrived. Didn't take them long to get on the job."

I nodded, only half listening as I opened the notebook.

"Okay, I'll heat up some soup. Yell if you need me."

By the time he walked through the kitchen door, I knew the notebook was Annabeth's journal. Within minutes I was caught up in the intimate details of her life.

When Dr. Hopkins returned from the kitchen with two bowls of soup, I was mesmerized. The entries in Annabeth's journal began years before she moved to Atlanta. Neeley was right. Annabeth was born and raised in Ludowici in Southeast Georgia. She was—to put it simply—a country girl. She was only 8 years old when her father died in a tractor accident. Her mother remarried two years later to a mill worker.

"I hope you like tomato," said Dr. Hopkins, sitting down beside me. "That's all I could find. My wife and Justin are visiting her parents. When Bridget returns—and they should be home any minute—she can fix you something better to eat."

Reluctantly, I pulled myself away from the journal and reached for the steaming mug of tomato soup. "Tomato soup is fine. Thank you," I said and smiled up at him, before turning back to my reading.

"How about another cup of tea?"

Actually what I wanted was a Cherry Coke and the chance to read Annabeth's journal without interruption.

"Annabeth? Lindsey?"

I snapped my head up from the journal. "What?"

"Another cup of tea?"

"Oh . . . I'm sorry, it's just . . . uh, sure . . . please." I turned back to the journal.

While he was gone, I discovered Annabeth's favorite subjects in middle school were math, science, and PE. She played girls' basketball, went out for track, and was a member of the science club. A fairly happy life until her mother remarried. I was so caught up in Annabeth's life, I did not hear Dr. Hopkins return until he waved another cup of tea under my nose.

"What's in the notebook that has you hanging on every word?" he asked, trying unsuccessfully to read over my shoulder. "A list of her clients? Drug dealers?"

"It's her personal diary." *Intimate details of her sad, pathetic life.*

"Diary of a hooker?" Dr. Hopkins smiled. "That must be interesting reading."

I stared at him. "Not what you think. Annabeth was born and raised in a small South Georgia town."

"Not enough action for her there, so she moved to 'Hotlanta'?"

I sighed in exasperation. "No, too much attention from a stepfather who molested her." I picked up the journal and turned the page. "When she told her mother, her stepfather denied everything. Let me read you something." I turned back several pages. "Listen to this."

Monday, June 15—Ever since the pool party at Aunt Lola's, Roger has been acting strange. I wore the new two-piece Mama bought me at Walmart. Slime green with pink polka-dots. When I pulled off my cover-up, I thought Roger's eyes would pop out of his head. I overheard him tell Mama I looked 16. Later, when everyone was headed to the kitchen to fix their burgers, Roger walked up to me in the living room where I was reading about Daniel Radcliffe in *Entertainment Weekly*. He grabbed my foot and used it to massage his crotch for two seconds before Aunt Lola came in and asked if we weren't going to eat. Roger, still holding my foot, turned to Lola, "Of course we are, Sweet Lady. I was just telling Annabeth that she had long legs like her mama." I wasn't sure what to make of what had happened, but I had a very uneasy feeling in my stomach.

Saturday, June 20—I wish now I'd told Mama about the foot incident at Aunt Lola's. Tonight, as I was walking down the hall toward my room, Roger stepped out of the bathroom in front of me—buck naked. I screamed. Roger covered himself with a towel just as Mama ran out of the living room. "What's going on out here?" Roger laughed, as I rushed by him into my room. "Weren't nothing. Annabeth startled me and I dropped my towel, that's all. Guess she never saw a naked man before." I slammed my door.

Wednesday, June 24—I hate him! I should have locked my door as soon as Mama left for the Piggly Wiggly. She hadn't been gone ten minutes before Roger was sitting butt naked next to me on my bed. I yelled for him to get out, but he just grinned. "Want to feel Mr. Willy?" Before I could scream "NO!" he grabbed my hand and forced it around his thing. It felt warm, damp, and sticky. I gagged and threw up Mama's spaghetti and meatballs all over him. He shoved me aside. "Look what you done!" After he ran out of the room, I locked the door behind him.

He was beating on my door in a few minutes. When I told him I was going to tell Mama, he said she wouldn't believe me because I was nothing but a slut who came onto *men. I sat down on the floor and cried. Later, after Mama's car pulled into the drive, I could hear Roger running his mouth. Then Mama was in my room, and I told her what had happened. How he made me touch him and everything. "Stop lying, Annabeth! Roger told me how you tricked him into coming into your room. How you forced yourself on him." Nothing I could say would convince her otherwise. I hate him! I want to kill him! I'm scared, and I don't know what to do.*

I paused and looked up at Dr. Hopkins. "She was only 12 years old when she wrote this. A middle schooler." I looked up at him. "How could a mother not believe her own child?"

Dr. Hopkins shook his head. "You'd be surprised how often a woman decides to believe the man who supports her rather than her own daughter. Poverty is an awful thing.

I shook my head and turned back to the diary. "Annabeth took money from her mother's purse and bought a bus ticket to Atlanta. Tony found her hungry, homeless, and begging in Piedmont Park." I was so focused on Annabeth's story, I didn't notice that Dr. Hopkins had left the room.

August 1—Tony's been very kind to me. Some of his friends are scary, but Atlanta is exciting! He said he can find work for me. Maybe working at the Varsity or Punk's Bar-B-Q."

I turned the page and scanned the writing.

August 18—Tony gave me some pills today. They make me feel really, really good. We made love. Tony loves me, and I love him. Maybe we'll get married.

August 27—Tony says if I truly love him, then I will have sex with his friends and make us some money. He says he has to pay extra for my food and stuff. That I need to contribute. I don't understand. If Tony really loves me, why would he want to let his friends have sex with me?

August 28—Today Tony made me move out of his place into an apartment with another girl named Neeley Hill. We share a mattress on the floor. I begged Tony to let me move back. I said I would be good. But he just laughed. I told him I wanted to go home, but Tony said my mother didn't want her slutty daughter back.

August 30—Since I have no money for a bus ticket, I decided to hitchhike home. Neeley said it was a bad idea. I should have listened to her. Tony's friend Dante—actually his bodyguard—found me and dragged me back. Tony beat me with his belt so badly I couldn't get out of bed the next day. Tony said he was sorry that I made him do it. He said he was very disappointed at my behavior after everything he'd done for me. Then he hugged me and told me how much he loved me. That I was his best girl. That he had invested more money in me than any of the others. And that if I ever crossed him, again, he'd kill me.

September 8—If only I could get my hands on some money, but that is impossible. Neeley told me that Tony posts his girls' photos online on sites like Craigslist and Backpage.com. Clients choose which girl they want and pay Tony up front. Then Dante takes the "chosen one" to the client. I asked Tony about getting some of the money, but he says I'm too young to hold onto money. He says he will take care of all of my needs, as long as I do as he says. I hate my life!"

A tear rolled down my cheek. "Poor Annabeth. How awful!" And now I'm in her miserable body. I began to sob.

Suddenly Justin was sitting beside me. "You all right?" He touched my shoulder, but I pushed him away.

"What are you doing?" I glared at him. "Leave me alone." I wiped my eyes on my sleeve.

"Justin, sweetheart, what are you doing?"

I looked up at an attractive woman wearing jeans and a plaid shirt. Freckles splattered across her make-up-free face, which was framed by short, ash-brown curls. She smiled and extended her hand. "Hello, I'm Bridget Hopkins. You must be Annabeth?"

I opened my mouth to correct her, but changed my mind. I grabbed her hand and shook it. "Nice to meet you, Mrs. Hopkins."

"Has Justin been bothering you?" She raised her eyebrow in his direction.

He jumped to his feet. "Mom!"

My eyes locked with Justin's. Here was my chance to get a little payback.

"Justin! I told you to stay in your room." Dr. Hopkins walked out of the kitchen with a glass of water and two pill bottles.

With a brief glance back at me, Justin strode out of the room.

"Annabeth, the guest room is ready for you." Then Bridget smiled at me, and two dimples indented her cheeks. "I laid out clean towels on your bed. Maybe in the morning after you've had a good night's rest, we can chat. I hope you'll excuse me for hurrying off, but I'm about to drop. I've been driving for four hours and I'm dead." She smiled her dimpled smile, again. "Good night!"

I smiled and nodded as she left. Too bad I wouldn't be here in the morning for breakfast.

Dr. Hopkins placed the water on the table. "It's time for your drugs," he said, shaking out two pills into my hand.

"Maybe I don't want any." Would these pills knock me out? I had plans. I couldn't afford to sleep.

"Trust me, you'll want these. The pills in this bottle subdue your drug withdrawal symptoms. The pills in the other bottle are an antibiotic for your infection."

I accepted the pills and swallowed them with the water. I didn't want any more chills and stomach cramps, that was for sure.

Dr. Hopkins left the pill bottles on the table and carried the soup mugs back into the kitchen.

I grabbed both bottles and dropped them into the backpack with the key. When Dr. Hopkins returned, I was lying on the sofa with my eyes closed. He sat on the edge of the sofa and grabbed my wrist. I snatched it away from him.

"I need to check your pulse."

Reluctantly, I gave him back my wrist. As his fingers pressed gently into my wrist, he checked his watch. He reached into his doctor's bag, took out a blood pressure cuff, wrapped it around my arm, and began pumping it up. The cold stethoscope disc pressed against the inside of my elbow. As the pressure of the cuff built tighter and tighter, it felt like my arm was being amputated. Then I heard the sudden hiss of released air and the tightness slowly eased. He quickly removed the cuff, folded it up, and put it in his bag. "Blood pressure is 118 over 70. I think you'll live."

I closed my eyes and tried to separate myself from the damaged body on the sofa. I thought about Rachel and the plans we'd made for after the state championship game. Had she or Dad gone with me in the ambulance to the hospital? Did they cry when they found out I had died? Then I pictured myself in my graduation gown, marching into the school auditorium, walking up on stage to receive my diploma. I saw myself posing with Rachel for photos. Dad kept focusing his digital camera and snapping at least a dozen photos, documenting our graduation antics. Then we were off to the big graduation party that I worked so hard to plan.

"Let me show you to the guest room." Dr. Hopkins stood up and offered me his hand.

I opened my eyes and shook my head. "Thanks, but I can do this by myself." I threw my legs over the side of the sofa and stood up.

"Excellent. After a good night's sleep, I bet you'll feel like a new person." Dr. Hopkins picked up Annabeth's backpack and led me down the hallway. The guest bedroom was small and contained only a queen-sized bed, covered with ruffled, fluffy pillows, and a couple of small tables with tiffany lamps. He turned on one of the lamps and set the backpack on the bed. "If you need anything, our room is on the other side of the kitchen. Good night."

I closed the door behind him and turned the lock until it clicked. I didn't want Justin coming in during the night for a visit. Pressing my forehead against the door, I tried to suppress a sob. Then out of nowhere, somebody grabbed my shoulder from behind. I struck back with my elbow and connected with ribs and flesh.

"Ow!" yelled Justin, rubbing his side. "Why'd you do that?"

I stared at him angrily, my heart racing and pounding in my chest. I was relieved he wasn't Tony—here to slit my throat—but angry that Justin was in my room. He must have been hiding behind the door. "What are you doing in here?"

"Waiting on you. You may have my dad convinced that you're Lindsey Anderson, but you can't fool me. I know the truth." He turned on the bedside lamp. "And I'm gonna out you."

CHAPTER THIRTEEN
INTO THE FIRE

I blinked my eyes in the bright light. Justin Hopkins was going to "out" me? I didn't think so. Who did he think he was? "Ha! You can't 'out' me, because I'm going to 'out' you!"

His eyes widened. "What?" He looked confused and a little bit fearful.

Was I ever going to take pleasure in bringing him down! "I bet Mr. Otis would love to know who dropped yellow phosphorous into the trash can and smoked the chemistry class into the hall." I had not said anything at the time, because I was happy to have the class end early. I really hated that class. It was the worst class at East Lake High. Everybody said so. Well, okay, they said that about American History, too. But chemistry was the absolute worst.

"How did you—?"

"And I know you super-glued Miss Wallington's coffee cup to her desk."

Justin frowned so hard his eyebrows kissed over the bridge of his nose.

I lowered my voice. "I saw you hide the glue tube in your peanut butter sandwich before she searched everybody's backpack. You should be glad she didn't take a bite out of your lunch." I couldn't help but smirk.

Strange gurgling sounds came from Justin's throat. He backed up against the wall and slowly slid down to the floor, staring at me like I had sprouted an extra head. "Only the real Lindsey would know that." His mouth opened and closed. "That's not possible," he said hoarsely. "You're not really . . ." He swallowed hard. "Lindsey?"

"Yeah, unfortunately," I whispered and sat down on the bed. "And now my life totally sucks." Then my emotional dam cracked and, even though I bit my tongue and dug my fingernails into my palms, I began to cry.

"Freaking unbelievable!" Keeping his distance, Justin grabbed a tissue box off the vanity and threw it at me.

I caught the box and snatched out a tissue. "Thanks." I said with a sniff and blew my nose loudly. "Sorry I'm having a sappy moment."

Justin plopped on the opposite end of the bed, his entire body trembling. For a long time, we stared at each other in silence, with only the sounds of me sniffing and Justin gulping down mouthfuls of air. Funny, but all the animosity I had felt for him melted away.

"Man, oh, man!" Justin finally found his voice. "Is this like one of those old body-switching movies? Like *Freaky Friday* or *It's a Boy Girl Thing* or . . ." His face turned pale. He blinked and rubbed the back of his neck. "Oh, no! Your dad had your body cremated. You can't even get your own body back. What a bummer! Bet that really sucks!"

"Yes, Justin, that really sucks!" How insensitive could one guy be? My eyes stung from fighting back the tears. "My life's over. My father thinks I'm a psycho. My best friend thinks I'm dead. I'm graduating posthumously. And here I sit in the body of a teen hooker, running from ghost busters, a drug-dealing pimp, and murderers."

"Not to mention Family and Children's Services."

"What?"

"You didn't know?"

I held my breath.

"DFACS wants you in foster care by the end of the week."

I bit down on my knuckles and whimpered. *If* I escaped getting murdered by Tony and dissected by parapsychologists, I would become a foster child. My life double-sucked.

Justin reached over and gingerly touched my shoulder. "I'm sorry."

I pulled back from him. "Don't touch me!" In spite of all his "love" notes, I had never had any feelings for him. My friends found him comical whenever he made goo-goo eyes at me. But their laughter never dissuaded or deterred him. "Justin, I'm sorry, but I just don't like you. You're a child. You're too young for me."

He looked down at his hands. His shoulders sagged. "I know," he whispered.

"Then why do you keep harassing me?" Did he just blush? "Did you know that Hatchet Man made me pick up every single empty Cherry Coke can you stuffed in my locker? You were the culprit who did that, weren't you?"

He squirmed and looked uncomfortable. "I wasn't trying to be mean. I thought you'd get a big laugh out of it. I wanted your birthday to be memorable. I wanted you to know you're special to me."

I stared at him. "*Holy crap*, Justin, when you like somebody, you don't do stupid things to them."

"I was only trying to get your attention." He avoided eye contact and rubbed the back of his neck.

"You got my attention all right—negative attention." I bowed my head and shook it slowly from side to side. "Justin, you need to find a girl your own age. Someone who appreciates you for who you are."

"Who am I?"

I frowned. I didn't even know who I was. I only know I'm not myself today. How could I answer his question? "Justin, everyone knows who you are. You make everybody laugh." But were we laughing at him or with him? He was the class clown and prankster. Since the beginning of our senior year, he had gotten detention four times for disrupting class.

Justin's nose twitched. "Did I ever make you laugh?"

I smiled, as I remembered. "Last spring when you did the imitation of Coach Aubrey and he was standing right behind you."

He banged the palm of his hand against his forehead. "Jeez! My most embarrassing moment. Thank goodness the coach thought it was funny, too!

I giggled. It felt good. "I was glad for once not to be the butt of your joke."

Justin's head shot up. His blue eyes locked on mine. "I'm sorry if the way I acted bugged you."

I nodded. Maybe he wasn't such a bad kid after all. "Guess you won't be writing me any more love notes?"

"Yeah," he said softly. "Because you aren't the girl of my dreams any more. She's gone forever."

Yeah, burned to a crisp in the oven. I sighed loudly. "I'm not exactly happy about that either."

Justin frowned. "I guess it sucks for both of us. But you know, there is a bright side here."

I scowled at him. "A bright side? What? That I'm alive and Annabeth isn't? That I lost the body I've inhabited for 18 years?" The tears began anew.

He slid off the bed. "Lindsey, listen to me."

Just when I was beginning to think he might not be a total jerk. "Justin, there is no bright side here!"

"Wait and listen for two minutes."

I sighed and sniffed. "Thirty seconds. Then you have to leave." *Because I have other plans.*

He took a deep breath. "Think of all the people in the world who would love to wake up younger. Who would like a re-do."

"Yeah, any movie star over forty. What's your point?"

He gave me a mischievous smile. "Your situation could be worse."

"Really? I don't think so." I propped my chin up with my hand. "Enlighten me."

Justin stretched out on the bed on his side facing me. "What if Annabeth were a really old woman with dentures and a walker?"

My spine stiffened. "This isn't funny, Justin. I want my life back. I want to be me, again." I buried my face in the pillow.

He reached out and touched my shoulder. "I wish I had a magic wand to wave over you and make everything back the way it was."

I wished that, too.

He pulled me towards him, and I didn't resist. I needed to be comforted. Dad wasn't here, but Justin was.

"Everything is going to be all right," he said softly. "You need to make the best of this. You have a new life and a new body."

"But I don't want this life," I blubbered. "I don't want this body. It's all worn-out. It's public property. And people are trying to kill it!"

He grimaced. "Yeah, but aside from that, you have an opportunity here."

"You see this as an opportunity?" *Had he gone mad?*

"Lindsey, did you ever wish you could start high school all over again, but with everything you've learned? You know, all of those life experiences that make you a wiser, better person?" He gently lifted my chin with his finger. It gave me a tingly feeling in my stomach. *Holy crap, Lindsey, remember that you detest this boy!*

"You mean like Mr. Olsen's tests come straight from the text book? And Danielle Fortson and Rosa Demarco will fall over if you stand up to them? And having a few close friends you can really count on in a crisis is better than having 300 shallow friends on Facebook?"

"Exactly! You have learned what is really important in life. You can do things differently a second time around. Think about it."

I rubbed my eyes and massaged the bridge of my nose wearily, trying to understand Justin's point. "Well, okay, I guess I could learn to play the clarinet and join the marching band." I'd always envied the camaraderie among the band members. "So where are you going with this?"

"Do I have to spell it out for you?"

I frowned. I wasn't getting this. Who in their right mind would want to repeat four years of high school? Who indeed? I chewed my bottom lip. This body is only 14 years old. If I did high school all over again, would I do anything differently? How would I act? Would I become friends with a different circle of kids? Would I join different organizations? Would I take different classes? My brain was going on overload.

Justin looked at me with this goofy expression on his face. "Would you be Homecoming Queen or a Varsity cheerleader or a total geek?"

I plopped myself against the pillows and pictured myself in this body on the first day of school. Scratch Homecoming Queen. This body was too scrawny for that. "Okay, so I'd be a freshman who already knew all the ins and outs of high school. You're thinking I wouldn't have any freshman insecurities?"

Justin grinned. "Now you're getting it."

I closed my eyes. Let me think about this. I could come up with winning projects for the science fair and become the champion math problem-solver. Would it be possible to make a perfect score on the SAT or get college credit for Advanced Placement classes or win an academic scholarship to college? My eyes popped open and I sat up, staring down at Jason. A glimmer of understanding twitched my lips. Justin smiled and nodded. I could do this. I could do my life all over again in Annabeth's body and make it even better than before.

CHAPTER FOURTEEN
TRYING HARD

Hours after Justin slipped out of my room, I lay awake on the bed. My brain was in overdrive, plotting a new plan of action. The house was quiet. But from outside I heard strange noises—like singing. I slipped out of bed and knelt next to the bedroom window, which faced the street. Two men stumbled down the sidewalk, approaching the parked patrol car from the rear. Each man held onto the other for support, loudly singing some tune off-key.

If Dr. Hopkins or his wife or Justin were awakened, my plans would be ruined. I prayed that the policeman would make them shut up. Maybe he could arrest them for disturbing the peace. It was almost 4 a.m. The entire neighborhood had to be asleep.

I tiptoed to the bedroom door and listened for any sounds. Hearing nothing, I grabbed the pair of disgusting zebra-print leggings from Annabeth's backpack and put them on. I tried not to gag. Wincing from the tenderness in my rib cage, I pulled a red tank top over my head and added the long-sleeved denim shirt for warmth. Anyone who saw me would probably think I was just another one of those girls who hang out on Metropolitan Parkway.

I felt really bad about sneaking out on Dr. Hopkins, but I had to leave. Dr. McCracken wouldn't be happy about this either, but I needed to confront Dad and Rachel. If I could see both of them face to face, then surely somehow, I could convince them it was really me.

I didn't know why I was worried about the doctors anyway. All they cared about was keeping me away from the "ghostbusters." Heaven forbid the hospital should get any bad publicity. Of course, there was also the little matter of that murderous Tony and Dante. Not to mention a foster home waiting with my name on it. But I would be safe if I made it home to Dad. Or should I leave the country until everything blows over? Nope, scratch that. No money. No passport.

As for shoes . . . hmm . . . the stiletto heels were out. Tennis shoes—even dirty, smelly ones—were more practical. Not shoes I would normally wear. I hefted Annabeth's backpack over my shoulder and quietly unlocked the bedroom window, raising it as high as I could. Thank goodness it wasn't a long drop from the window ledge to the ground. Hiding behind a sticky holly bush, I silently cursed the prickly leaves that stabbed me through my clothes.

Fully focused on the two singing drunks, I didn't notice a crouching figure behind the large hydrangea bush until he crawled out.

"Leaving without me?" the figure in the shadows whispered.

"Justin!" My breath hissed through my teeth. "What are you doing here?" I certainly didn't need a body guard.

"Waiting on you. I knew you'd be slipping out sooner or later."

Justin stepped closer. I could feel the warmth from his body and smell his citrus-lime bath soap. I swallowed hard and quickly reminded myself that this was the same person who ran my gym clothes up the flag pole.

"Let me guess where you're going, Lindsey. You're headed home to find your dad?"

Before I could reply, one of the drunks—short and stocky— punched the other one—tall and thin with copper-colored dreadlocks. The blow to his chin knocked him flat on his back. Then the short man began hitting him with his fists.

"Shhhh," I whispered to Justin and pointed across the street. I half-crawled to the yard next door and hid behind an oak tree. Justin followed my lead. We watched as a policeman jumped out of the patrol car.

"Break it up! Stand up and place your hands on your head!" the policeman yelled, reaching down and grabbing the shoulder of the bald man on top. But the guy with the dreadlocks, who was lying on the ground, kicked and tripped the policeman.

Oh, this was not going well. I watched in horror as the two men overpowered the policeman, beating and kicking him until he lay unmoving on the ground. "Do you have a cell phone?" I asked Justin.

Justin grabbed his pocket and muttered something under his breath. "It's on the charger."

Oh great, now what? I watched the two men drag the policeman to his patrol car and prop him behind the steering wheel. From outside the car, he appeared to be dozing.

An icy cold spread throughout my body. *Holy crap!* "Those two men are Tony and Dante." I shivered. "They're here looking for me."

Justin edged closer to me. "Who? How do you know them?"

"That Atlanta police detective showed me photos of them. I don't know them, but Annabeth did. She stole Tony's drug money. Dante is his body guard."

"Is Tony the man who beat you—uh—Annabeth's body?"

"I'm afraid so." Was this going to complicate everything? I knew I should have left two hours ago. Now what? Still behind the oak tree, we watched the men cross the Hopkins' front yard and crouch behind a large bush near the front door.

"Gotta warn my parents," Justin said, rising to his feet. "You check on the policeman and call for help on his radio."

"Okay." I couldn't see his face well in the darkness, but I could hear the emotion in his voice. "Be careful."

"You, too. Wait for me."

"Of course," I whispered, but I knew I wouldn't stick around and wait to be murdered. I scurried closer to the sidewalk and didn't look back, even when I heard the sound of breaking glass. Justin and his parents would be all right. I was the one Tony wanted.

Shaking all over, I reached the policeman as he stumbled from the patrol car. Hanging onto the open car door, he tried to stand up. "Officer, are you okay?" He didn't look like it. His face and shirt were bloody. One eye was swollen shut, and the other looked at me unsteadily.

"Can I call for help?" I asked. My heart pounded in my chest and my side hurt like it was splitting open.

"I did," he mumbled. "Backup's coming." He stumbled and slid down the side of the car, until he was sitting on the ground. His eyes closed; his head lolled sideways.

Okay, Lindsey, you're the one who spent two Saturdays taking First Aid and CPR with the Red Cross. Do something. I knelt on the ground beside the policeman and shook him. "Mister, can you hear me?" His eyes flickered. His chest rose up and down. That was good. I didn't want to do any mouth-to-mouth thing, if he was still breathing. In the distance I heard sirens. I looked across the street at Justin's house, but couldn't see or hear anything.

When I turned back, I saw flashing blue lights moving up the street. I looked down at the policeman and squeezed his shoulder. "Your friends are here. You're going to be all right. I have to go." He lifted his head and rolled his one good eye in silent protest, but I didn't need to get waylaid by the police. As I slipped down the street into the darkness, I could hear sirens, tires screeching, and men shouting. I didn't look back.

• • • • •

It wasn't until I reached the closest bus stop on Piedmont, that I realized someone was about 100 feet behind me. Fortunately, a MARTA bus pulled up and opened its doors. Maybe my luck was changing. But as I stepped into the bus, I saw a man with dreadlocks closing in, his face distorted in rage.

"Nobody screws with Tony!" he yelled.

My heart dropped, and my stomach lurched. Turning to the young bus driver—a Will Smith look-a-like—I yelled, "Get out of here."

The bus driver pointed to Tony, who had almost reached the bus. "Maybe he wants a ride, too."

I started shaking his arm and shrieking. "No, he wants to kill me! Go, go, go!"

His black eyes widening, the bus driver shut the door and pulled away from the curb. "What did you do to him?"

I tapped Annabeth's MARTA Breeze Card on the blue target and fell back into the seat behind the driver. A scruffy old man with shoulder-length gray hair and a long white beard sat in the back of the bus. Wearing a dirty, red-knit cap pulled down over his ears, he saluted me with a bottle in a brown paper bag and smiled a toothless grin.

"That man chasing me beat up a policeman."

"I knew he was trouble as soon as I laid eyes on him." He looked at my reflection in his rearview mirror. "You okay, Miss?"

"So far." And I hoped that Justin and his parents were okay, too.

Tony, gold-chain necklaces flapping around his neck, raced alongside the bus, hitting the door with his fists. "Stop the damn bus!" he screamed.

"Not a nice way to talk to a public servant," said the driver.

As the bus pulled away from Tony, a white Cadillac screeched to a halt behind us. The passenger door flung open and Tony hopped in.

"See," said the driver, "I took care of him, didn't I?"

"I don't think we've seen the last of him." My stomach quivered. I didn't see how this bus could outrun a Cadillac. I felt like a hunted rabbit hiding in a glass fox hole.

"Don't you worry, little lady, Leo's been driving this bus for two years, seven months, two weeks and three days without an accident."

"These men are bad guys, Leo." I immediately thought about what they did to Annabeth and Neeley, and the policeman. As the Cadillac came up fast on the bus's rear, I wished I were a passenger in a bullet-proof Hummer. Or even the Pope Mobile. "If you want another day without a mishap, Leo, I'd call for help."

Leo looked in his side mirror and sped up.

I gasped when the Cadillac pulled up alongside the bus driver's window. The car's passenger window lowered and Tony leaned out, waving his gun and shouting. "Pull over! NOW!"

I crouched down in my seat. Could my life get any worse?

Leo turned the bus sharply to the left, striking the side of the Cadillac and sending it veering across the street, where it sideswiped three parked cars. The impact knocked me over.

The bearded man lost control of his bottle, which flew up in the air and slammed against the window, before bouncing down the aisle. "Wee, doggies!" he yelled and grinned like a lunatic.

Leo, meanwhile, snatched up his radio mike. "Dispatch, this is Leo. I'm being attacked by a maniac! I'm on Piedmont heading out. Send help!" He looked in his rearview mirror at me. "You all right?"

I was shaking all over. I swallowed hard and nodded. "For now." But for how much longer? If Tony got on this bus, I was dead. Maybe it wouldn't be too bad. I'd already died once and didn't remember anything about it.

"Don't you worry, Miss. I served in Iraq, and I'm not going down without a fight."

As the Cadillac headed straight for the bus, Leo's words brought me no comfort. Tony leaned out of the car window and fired his gun. I ducked, window glass shattering around me.

"Yippee aye oh, little doggies!" screamed the drunk.

"Idiot!" screamed Leo, swerving the bus into the Cadillac, again.

The collision sent me sprawling face down on the floor. I screamed.

"Yahoo!" yelled the man from the rear of the bus.

Brakes squealed, another shot was fired, and Leo grunted, as the bus sideswiped the Cadillac, one more time. The Cadillac swerved and crashed into a telephone pole. The impact of the bus against the Cadillac rolled me over onto my back."

When I heard Leo cry out, "He got me," I crawled over to him. Blood oozed down his white shirt sleeve. His right arm flopped uselessly at his side. He leaned in his seat, clinging to the large steering wheel for support. I pulled myself up beside him, as the bus slowly came to a halt at the 14th Street intersection. "Let me help you," I said, applying pressure to his wound. That First Aid class was really paying off today.

"I got this," Leo said, pushing my hand away. "Get out while you can."

I turned my head and saw Tony and Dante crawling out of the wrecked Cadillac. They kept going like Energizer bunnies. "We have to stop the bleeding, Leo" I said.

Leo pressed his own hand over the wound. "Latonya's sending help. See that yellow cab pulling up to the light?"

I looked over at the taxi and nodded.

"It's my friend Barney. Tell him Leo sent you." He pulled the lever and opened the door.

I hesitated. I had messed up his perfect record after all.

"Go!"

I stumbled off the bus. My body hurt all over, but I willed myself to keep going. I reached the taxi just as the light changed and it began rolling away. "Barney!" I screamed.

CHAPTER FIFTEEN
HOME SWEET HOME

Brakes squealed as the taxi stopped, and the driver leaned over and lowered the passenger window. "Do I know you?" he asked warily.

"Leo sent me. See his bus?" I pointed behind me. Leo waved his good arm out the window. The bearded drunk stumbled outside the bus, swaying unsteadily and waving his bottle wildly in the air. "Hasta la vista, baby!"

Barney followed my finger and relaxed. He unlocked the door. "Hop in. How's Leo?"

I slid across the backseat, slammed the door shut, and looked back to see Tony and Dante bolting past the bus. They ran into the drunk, who lost his balance and toppled to the asphalt, knocking both men down. But only briefly. Then Tony and Dante were back on their feet and in pursuit of Barney's taxi.

"Uh, could you get going? Really fast! See, Leo isn't doing so well." My voice quaked. "See the two men heading this way? They shot Leo and now they're coming for me."

Barney stomped the gas pedal to the floor. With tires squealing, the taxi lunged around the corner onto 14th Street, throwing me backwards in the seat. I groped for my seat belt and clicked it into place.

Tony, his mass of dreadlocks flapping around his face, grabbed the handle on the taxi's passenger door, but found it locked. He screamed out some really bad words, as we left him in the middle of the street. A man in an approaching black BMW blew his horn and swerved to avoid hitting Tony and Dante. But as we drove out of sight, I saw the two men crawling on top of the BMW.

Barney must have been a NASCAR driver in another life. It was a white-knuckle ride through Midtown with tires squealing as we slid around corners. Even with my seat belt on, I couldn't sit up straight, and the belt kept digging into my tender spots. Finally, Barney slowed down to just above the speed limit, and I was able to breathe. Compared to the hours since I'd died on the soccer field, the first 18 years of my life had been boring. I just didn't realize it at the time I was living it.

Barney looked in his rearview mirror at me. "Where to, little lady?"

"The Darlington Terrace, please." The high-rise apartments that had been my home for 18 years.

Barney nodded and cut across two lanes of traffic to make a left turn onto Northside Drive.

I took a deep breath and let it out slowly, trying to get the muscles in my shoulders and neck to release some of the tension. A new morning was breaking, the street traffic picked up as the sun rose, and I suddenly realized we were only minutes away from my apartment. How would Dad react when he saw me? And what would I say to him?

Somewhere on Northside Drive, at a busy intersection, I saw a BMW stopped at the light. I sucked in my breath with an audible gasp.

"What?" asked Barney, looking at me in his rearview mirror.

Looking out the rear window, I watched the BMW tear around the corner. "See that BMW pulling out of the intersection?"

"Yeah . . . three cars back. Is it those bad guys? Don't worry, if it's them, they won't be back there long." He pressed his foot down on the gas, throwing me back against the seat. Like on an amusement park ride, only I wasn't amused.

Five minutes later, Barney deposited me in front of my apartment building. I fumbled through the backpack for cash. "No charge, Miss," he barked at me. "You're the most exciting passenger I ever had. Now I gotta go check on Leo!"

I barely closed the cab door before Barney sped off, making a U-turn on two wheels. Hobbling across the sidewalk to the double-glass door entrance, I was brought up short by the appearance of our night security guard Morris. If only it had been Leroy. Morris, who was retired from the Atlanta PD, would be difficult to cajole into letting a stranger into the building. As I tried to decide how best to get past Morris, I heard a commotion behind me. I turned and saw Tony and Dante yelling and jumping out of the BMW.

No time to think now. I pushed through the doors and literally fell into the arms of Morris. "Help!" I cried, breathing hard, like I was scared out of my mind. And I was. "Two men are trying to kill me." Tears rolled down my cheeks. I bit my bottom lip and thought of Dad standing over my dead body.

Morris glanced outside and drew his service revolver, while pushing me behind him. I had never seen him respond so fast to anything. He moved up a notch in my security guard book.

When Tony and Dante burst through the double doors into the lobby, Morris was ready and waiting. "Halt right there, gentlemen. This is private property! Suppose you turn around and leave quietly, so I don't have to call the police."

Not waiting to see who blinked first, I hurried around the corner of the lobby to the building's two elevators. The one on the right was waiting with its doors open. I pressed the button for the 34th floor. As the elevator doors shut, I heard yelling in the lobby. I closed my eyes and said a prayer for Morris.

Shaking all over, I leaned against the side of the elevator. Could it move any slower? Finally, it reached my floor. The pain in my rib cage was getting worse, and my knees were shaking so badly, I could barely walk. Somehow, I made it down the hall to my apartment and rang the bell. Nothing. I rang it, again. Where could Dad be? Normally, he wouldn't get out of bed before 8 a.m. unless the building was on fire. I put my ear to the door, but heard nothing.

Just then the door opened across the hall, and my neighbor Mrs. Cooper stepped out with her three Cockapoos. A red beret, sitting on top of her wavy, snow-white hair, matched her red hand-knit sweater. I forced myself to smile. She was one of my favorite neighbors. "Good morning, Mrs. Cooper. Out walking the babies?" I knelt on the floor and hugged the dogs. "What happened to Gretchen's paw?" I asked, noticing it was bandaged.

Mrs. Cooper's frown turned into a smile. "Oh, my poor baby stepped on a piece of glass. Three stitches. Do I know you, child?"

"Yes, ma'am." I hesitated. No way was I going to tell her I was Lindsey. "Don't you remember me? I'm a friend of Lindsey's."

"No, Honey, my memory isn't what it used to be." She wiped her right eye with a pink, lacy hanky. "Terrible thing that happened to Lindsey, wasn't it?"

"Yes, ma'am, it really was." I looked down at another one of the dogs, while trying to keep my emotions in check. "That's a pretty bow in Snookums' hair, Mrs. Cooper. It matches her eyes perfectly."

"Why thank you, sweetie. What did you say you were doing here so early this morning?"

"Lindsey borrowed my best dress. Dr. Anderson promised he'd be here, so I could pick it up this morning. It looks like I missed him." I scratched Gretchen behind her ears. "I need that dress desperately." A tear rolled down my cheek. "Say, don't you have an extra key to their apartment? I know exactly where my dress is."

"Oh, sweetie, I don't know. Let me walk the babies, and we'll talk when I get back."

"I'd like to, but I have a job interview this morning. If I have to wear what I have on, I know I won't get the job."

Mrs. Cooper looked at the skin-tight, zebra-striped leggings and nodded in agreement. "Uh-huh, you're probably right about that, child. You might want to shampoo your hair and put on a little makeup, too." She reached into her purse and pulled out a key ring with a single key. "Here, dearie. I know Lindsey would want you to have your dress."

I gave the woman a hug. "Thank you, Mrs. Cooper. You're a dear!"

"Okay, honey, make sure you lock that door when you leave and give the key to Morris on the way out."

Yeah, I could do that, providing Morris was there to give it to.

As Mrs. Cooper made her way down the hall toward the elevators, I inserted the key in the lock and let myself into the apartment, closing the door softly behind me. From down the hallway, I could hear the elevator doors open—and male voices. A cold shiver went up and down my spine. I cracked the door and listened.

"Now what?" asked one man.

"I don't know," a second voice snapped back.

"We could blow open every door 'til we find her."

"Fool, put that gun away. This isn't some back alley. We'll stay right here and wait. Sooner or later she'll have to leave."

It was definitely Dante and Tony. I silently shut the door and turned the dead bolt. I would worry about them later. Right now, I was just happy to be home. I hugged myself and sighed blissfully, looking around the living room I thought I would never see, again. CNN Headline News—Dad's favorite news channel—blared from our new 55" LG HDTV.

I walked over to the display cabinet and picked up a photo of a much younger me standing between smiling parents. It had been taken on Amelia Island during the last vacation before my mom died. How I wished she were here now to talk to Dad and persuade him I really am his daughter. But what was it with this tall stack of packed boxes? Was Dad moving away? I opened one of the boxes marked "books." It was full of my old picture books, early chapter books, and books from middle school that had been stored in a hall closet. My ashes were barely cold, and Dad was already moving my stuff out? I couldn't believe it!

When I entered Dad's bedroom, the bathroom door was closed. I could hear the water running in the shower. I placed my hand on the doorknob, but changed my mind. Instead, I went to my bedroom. The room looked exactly like it did the evening I left for the championship game. My soccer trophies lined the shelves of one bookcase. Hanging on the wall over my desk was a photo of me and Rachel in our soccer uniforms. Everything in this room represented the happier times of my former body. A lump formed in my throat.

I pulled open my louvered closet doors. Thank goodness my clothes and shoes were intact. I should look decent when I confronted Dad, not like a teenage hooker. Too bad I didn't have time for a shower. The "bird baths" at the hospital were not that effective. I was probably starting to smell pretty ripe.

Quickly, I looked through the outfits in my closet, sliding them one by one, down the clothes rod. I settled on Dad's favorite outfit—cobalt blue trousers and a white silk blouse. Even before I looked in the mirror, I knew the blouse hung and bagged on my new thinner body. I buttoned and zipped the trousers, but they dropped around my ankles. I removed the clothes and dressed back into Annabeth's spandex pants. What was I going to do now? How much weight would I have to gain to fit into my own clothes?

Then I spotted my brown leather Coach bag on the chest of drawers and opened it, pulling out my wallet, driver's license, two credit cards—VISA and Macy's—and my key ring. I could always drive to the mall and buy new clothes that would fit this body. But if I'm supposed to be dead, would I be able to use my credit cards? I counted out the cash in my wallet: $48.07. That wouldn't buy much at Lenox Square. I could drive to Walmart, but what if someone recognized Annabeth's body? Spreading out the bills on top of my dresser, I heard movement behind me and swirled around. Dad, his hair still wet from the shower, stood there in a pair of black slacks.

"You!" Dad yelled. "How did you get in here?"

Caught off guard, I dropped several five-dollar bills on the floor. My heart racing, I bent over to pick them up, but Dad grabbed my wrist.

"Hand me that purse!" He shoved me backwards onto the bed and pried a twenty-dollar bill from my clenched fist.

I tried to free myself from his grip. "Dad, don't! You're hurting me."

He glanced at the clothes on the bed. "What are you doing with my daughter's things?" He released my wrist and reached for my cell phone lying on the bed next to my wallet. "I'm calling 911."

Collapsing to the floor at his feet, I grabbed Dad around his legs and wept. "No, Dad, don't! It's me, Lindsey. Please, believe me." I'd never groveled like this before. How pathetic! Is this what I was becoming?

Dad stared at me for a long time in silence. "You aren't my daughter. You need help." His breath came out in hoarse gasps.

My arms tightened around his legs, and I wouldn't let go.

"Stop that!" He reached down and tried to loosen my grip.

"Dad, listen! I really _am_ Lindsey. I passed out at the soccer game and woke up in this body." I looked up at his flushed and angry face. My stomach lurched.

Over the years I had seen my father angry for one reason or another. And plenty of those times he was angry at me—like the time I used a kitchen knife to break up a layer of sleet on the rooftop of his new Mercedes, leaving behind scratches and dents. But this was his most hateful look. The one reserved for the worst sorts of people, like the hit-and-run DUI who drove onto the sidewalk and killed our neighbor's young son or the three high school boys who burned down the free clinic.

How much more of this could I take? I could barely breathe and my chest hurt. Was I having a panic attack?

Dad grabbed me roughly by the upper arms and pulled me to my feet, shaking me furiously. "Why are you here?" he asked angrily. "Can't you leave me alone?"

I tried to free myself from his grip to no avail. "Stop, Dad! You're hurting me!"

But Dad wouldn't let go. "Who are you and what do you think you're doing?"

When I cried out, Dad released me, and I pulled away from him. Tears rolled down my cheeks from the pain in my arms and the ache in my heart. "I know you don't believe me, but Dr. Hopkins does. And Dr. McCracken, too."

"Then they're idiots! You're nothing but a con artist. I'll pay you to leave town. How much will it take?"

I swallowed the huge lump in my throat. "What can I say to convince you I'm your daughter?"

"Nothing!" He spat out the word. "Anything you say would be a lie! I don't have to stay here and listen to you." He spun around and walked toward the door.

I couldn't let him leave. Fighting to control my emotions, I spoke in a calm voice. "When I was six years old, you won me a red stuffed snake at Six Flags. I named him Charley. Remember? After a snake you owned when you were a boy." Dad stopped, but didn't turn around.

"Right after I got my driver's license, I skidded off the highway in a terrible rain storm into a ditch. Even though it was

3 a.m., you got out of bed when I called and helped me get my car back on the road. And you didn't yell at me once."

Dad's shoulders slumped.

"The night before I died, you said you hoped that one day I would make the Olympic Women's Soccer team. I still can, Dad. But it will have to be in this body. This is the only body I have now. Believe in me. I can do it, but you'll have to wait a little longer than you expected."

A strangled sob escaped from Dad's throat.

I placed my hand on his shoulder. "Shall I go on?" I asked him.

He turned to face me. "No," he whispered hoarsely. "That's enough."

He took my hand in his and looked into my eyes. The scent of Irish Spring soap from his shower swept over me. I wanted to grab him around the neck and hug him tight. I wanted to feel his arms around me. I wanted him to call out my name.

"What if I believe everything you're saying?" Dad asked, rubbing a finger over the back of my hand. "What if I say there's not a doubt in my mind that you're my daughter?"

My knees suddenly felt weak. I opened my mouth to speak, but he held up his hand. "No, let me finish. I'm a researcher. A scientist. I believe in facts. You're asking me to believe in something that's way out in left field."

I shook my head. "But Dad, don't you think I've been using the logic and analytical skills I inherited from you to try and figure this thing out? To try and understand what has happened to me? Do you think it has been easy for me to accept this?"

Dad dropped my hand and stepped back. "Don't you understand? You are <u>not</u> the daughter I knew and cherished for eighteen years." He wiped his eyes with the back of his hand and stared at me intently.

My heart seemed to leap from my chest. The blood rushed to my face. A sob escaped from my throat, as I looked away from Dad's piercing eyes.

"I can't accept what you're saying," Dad said quietly. "You are not my Lindsey."

Without another word, Dad turned and walked out of the bedroom. I stood in shock, frozen to the spot. Then suddenly all the anger and rage that had been festering under the surface boiled over. I ran after him, grabbed his arm and spun him around to face me. "Don't do this to me. I am your daughter, whether you want to admit it or not. You know how stubborn I can be. I inherited it from you. I'm not going to let this go. I would expect this from anyone else, but not from my own father!" I yelled at him.

Dad stuck his face in mine. Crimson color spread from underneath his collar and up his neck. "I'm sorry you inherited my stubbornness. It's not my fault!" His eyes widened and bulged. His face paled. His mouth hung open in silence. Suddenly his body snapped military straight.

I sucked in my breath. *Holy crap! Had Dad in some backhanded way acknowledged that I was Lindsey?* Was he conceding? I grabbed him around the waist.

Dad covered both ears with his hands and shut his eyes. "Don't say another word!" he hissed. "Go away! Leave me alone!" His voice broke.

"Dad, I'm telling the truth. Please! I love you so much!" I cried, as my body shook. "If you won't believe me, what am I going to do?"

"Get away from me." He pushed me away and held up my cell phone. "I am dialing 911. Leave now before the police arrive." But before Dad could call, the doorbell sounded.

I stopped sobbing. It had to be Tony and Dante.

With the phone at his ear, Dad pushed me aside and ran out of my room.

"No, Dad!" I screamed after him. Groaning from the pain, I stood up and stuffed the money, wallet, and keys into Annabeth's backpack. I wasn't going to wait to be shot in my own bedroom. Hugging the wall, I made my way to the living room and crouched behind the sofa. I stifled a gasp when I saw Justin standing in the open doorway. He looked okay except for a purple bruise on one cheek.

"Is she here or not, Dr. Anderson?" he asked Dad.

Justin had figured out where I was. Perhaps I had underestimated him.

"I need to talk to her, sir," he added.

"Yes, she's here."

"Does my father know?" Justin asked.

"No, but I've called the police just like I promised." He pointed to his boxer shorts. "I didn't even get a chance to get dressed. I stepped out of the shower, and there she was in Lindsey's room, going through her belongings."

"Where is she, sir?" he asked, stepping into the living room.

"Down the hall. Last door on the left."

Justin stepped forward. "If you hurt her . . ."

"I didn't touch her, Justin. She's one mixed-up, confused girl. She needs psychiatric help. What's your interest in her anyway?"

Oh, no, I was afraid to hear his answer. I bit my lip.

Justin shrugged.

Dad shook his head. "I see. She got to you, didn't she?"

Justin rubbed his chin. "Maybe. You don't believe her, do you?"

"Absolutely not. She had a complete meltdown when I wouldn't let her take Lindsey's clothes and money. The police should be here any minute."

I fought back the lump in my throat and crawled around the sofa to the pile of boxes near the open door. I couldn't believe that my own father—the man I looked up to and respected, the man who told me every night he loved me—would hand me over to the police.

Justin pushed past my Dad. "I don't understand you, Dr. Anderson."

"What's to understand? I step into my daughter's bedroom and find this schizophrenic, delusional girl rummaging through Lindsey's personal effects and claiming to be my daughter." Dad choked and wiped his eyes with the back of his hand. "I'm sorry. I can't deal with this."

He can't deal with this? I'm the one in the wrong body. I'm the one who should be thinking about graduation and soccer camp. I'm the one who wins the "My Life Sucks the Most Award."

Justin patted Dad's arm. "It's okay, Dr. Anderson. I understand. You're left-brained. You deal in facts and logic. This is not in your realm of possibility."

"It's scientifically impossible."

"Right," Justin took a step backwards toward my bedroom. "For what it's worth, I'm sure she didn't intentionally try to upset you. She only wants her life back."

I blinked back tears. If Justin believes who I am, why couldn't Dad? Then from my hiding spot, I noticed two figures stop in the open front door. With guns drawn, Tony and Dante rushed into the living room.

"Where is she?" Tony pointed his revolver at Dad and Justin.

Justin glared, his jaw clinched, but Dad's eyes glanced fleetingly toward the back of the apartment.

Thank goodness I wasn't in the bedroom.

Tony grinned and motioned with his head. "Dante, check it out."

Dad stepped in that direction, but Tony shoved him into the wall. "Uh-uh. You stay right here."

Now was the time for me to slip out the door unnoticed. Once Tony and Dante realized I was gone, they would leave, and Dad and Justin would be okay. I was the one whose life was in danger.

"Who are you?" Dad asked Tony.

"Shut up, I'm the only person here who gets to ask questions." Tony pointed his gun at Dad.

"Dr. Anderson, meet Tony, Annabeth's pimp. He wants to kill her," introduced Justin.

"Yeah," grinned Tony. "I'm her pimp, and I'm gonna kill her." He laughed nastily.

"Boss, she ain't here!" yelled Dante from the back of the apartment.

Tony jabbed the barrel of his revolver into Dad's neck. "Mister, are you messing with me?"

"Maybe she slipped out the door," Dante said.

And I had. Out the door, down the hall, and right into the elevator—just as Mrs. Cooper and her yipping Cockapoos exited.

"You better give me the key, dearie." She held out her hand. "Morris has deserted his post."

She looked at me expectantly. "Didn't you get your dress, child?" she asked, as I handed her the door key.

"No, ma'am, I didn't like the way it fit. I guess I'll have to wear what I have on. Thanks for your help." Looking behind Mrs. Cooper, I saw Tony and Dante burst out of our apartment.

Mrs. Cooper frowned and nudged her babies down the hallway.

As the elevator doors began to close, Tony and Dante collided with Mrs. Cooper and her Cockapoos. The dogs yelped; Mrs. Cooper screamed. My last view of Tony and Dante was of them tumbling to the floor—tangled in leashes and yipping dogs.

•   •   •   •   •

I exited the elevator in the basement where tenants parked their cars and let out a sigh of relief at the sight of my beloved yellow Mustang convertible in my personal parking space. Opening the door on the driver's side, I slid in and fastened my seat belt. Rachel and I had had plenty of good times in this Mustang, including our recent spring-break road trip to Savannah, where we stayed in Rachel's grandparents' cottage on Tybee Island.

A lump rose in my throat when I realized Annabeth's legs were too long for her knees to fit under the steering wheel. I slid the seat back as far as it would go, adjusted the rearview mirror, and inserted the key into the ignition, just as the second elevator opened. As soon as I saw Tony and Dante dash out, I ducked down in the seat and listened to them stampede past my car.

Slouched in the seat, I turned the key in the ignition and started the engine. Backing out of the parking space, I saw the men turn around and point their guns at me. My hands trembled on the steering wheel, and my knees shook. Tony and Dante stood between me and the exit.

Feeling like I was in the middle of an action-thriller movie, I pressed the gas pedal to the floor. The Mustang leaped forward, sending both men scurrying for safety. Tony shot at my car as it passed them, hitting my side-view mirror. The bullet ricocheted through the open window and grazed my forehead, causing me to nearly hit a new Mercedes as I exited the garage.

Eighteen years I had lived in Atlanta, and not once had I ever been a crime victim or been in fear of my life. Just my luck to get stuck in the body of a teenage girl being chased by murderers. Rubbing my stinging forehead, I felt something warm and sticky dribble down my face. I looked at the blood on my fingers and instantly felt nauseous and faint. How did I ever manage to dissect that pig in human biology class?

CHAPTER SIXTEEN
AND GOD CREATED GIRLFRIENDS

Standing in front of Rachel's home, I was able to look through the large floor-to-ceiling windows into the Adams' modern living room. I could see the family's white floor-to-ceiling book shelves, chrome floor lamps, chrome and glass coffee table, and poster-size Andy Warhol prints on the walls. And I could see my best friend Rachel curled up on the red leather sofa with a white fleecy throw.

Her parents' Lexus wasn't parked in the driveway. Thank goodness for that. It was going to be difficult enough just dealing with Rachel. But if I could convince Rachel that I was me in another body, then she would help me win over Dad. She would help me get my life back. I rang the doorbell and waited.

"Who is it?" Rachel's voice called out.

"Rachel," I yelled, "let me in," I said, wiping my face with the back of my hand. I didn't want the sight of blood oozing down my forehead to scare her. I was scared enough for both of us. I pressed my ear against the door and heard footsteps approaching.

"What do you want?" I heard Rachel's voice through the door.

"Rachel, please let me in." I leaned against the door. I knew she was looking through the peephole. My heart was beating so fast, I thought it was crawling up my throat. I took several deep breaths and willed myself to remain calm.

"Do I know you?" It sounded like her face was pressed against the door on the other side.

"Yes, I'm your friend. Please!" I had no problem sounding pathetic. I'd get down and grovel if necessary—although it definitely hadn't worked with Dad. I would do whatever it took to get through the front door. I held my breath and waited.

"I don't know you," she said, after a few seconds. "You should leave."

"Rachel, please." My chin quivered, as I let out a sob. "I've been shot. Help me." It was just a matter of time before she opened that door. I knew her well. She was a kind, sensitive person who took stray, injured dogs and cats to the vet and paid for their care. "You can't leave me out here to die, Rachel." Suddenly I felt overcome with nausea. Was it only my imagination or was it slowly getting dark? I guess my body had been running on an adrenaline high, because suddenly everything went black.

. . . . . .

Waking up face-down on Rachel's gritty concrete stoop was not one of my better moments. Rachel knelt beside me, holding my hand. She reeked of the body lotion I had given her for

Christmas—something by Burberry with a floral woody smell. And I thought it was too stinky for her to ever use.

"Are you all right? Do you live around here? Should I call your parents?"

Lifting my head slightly, I looked into my friend's pale, frightened face. She was wearing her favorite, black satin, kimono robe that her parents brought her from Japan. "No, no . . . water . . . just some water . . . please . . ."

Rachel brushed raven-black bangs away from her brown eyes. "I could call an ambulance."

"No, not necessary."

Rachel half-dragged, half-carried me into the living room and deposited me on the family's hard, red leather sofa. Good thing Annabeth was such a small, skinny person. Rachel would never have been able to drag my previous body inside the house.

"I'll be right back," she told me and headed for the kitchen.

As soon as she left, I stumbled to the more comfortable sofa on the other side of the room. I hated her leather sofa. It was cold to my butt in the winter and stuck to the back of my legs and thighs in the summer. I settled into comfy cushions, my eyes settling on a photo of me and Rachel on the end table. The photo was taken last month at her grandparents' beach cottage on Tybee Island. Two best friends, tan and mugging the camera. Our arms hanging loosely around each other's shoulders, we looked happy and carefree. We were the invincible "East Lake Bombers." A lump rose in my throat.

I closed my eyes and pretended this was a normal day. Any minute Rachel and I would be hanging out, gossiping, and enjoying each other's company. Maybe it's true what they say— you can't really appreciate something you have until you've lost it.

Rachel returned with a glass of water, a damp washcloth, and a first-aid kit. "Here," she said, stopping in mid-sentence, after noticing that I wasn't where she left me.

"Hey," I called out to her. "I'm over here. You know how I hate sitting on that cold leather sofa."

She turned and scowled. "What the——? I thought you were dying! That probably isn't blood at all—just catsup." She picked up her cell phone. "I'm calling the police."

That was the last thing I needed. My mind raced for the right words. "Don't be mean to me!"

"I'm sorry. What did you say? I'm being mean to you? Hold on just a minute. This is my house, and you're trespassing."

"I don't remember you ever being this testy." I raised myself to a sitting position and snatched the wet cloth out of Rachel's hand. "It's pretty bad when a bleeding teammate has to take care of her own self." I wiped the blood off my face and pointed to the raw crease on my forehead, next to my bandaged stitches. "See, no catsup."

Rachel leaned over and examined the area. "Omigosh! You _are_ hurt, but it's just a small wound." She stood up straight, her eyes narrowed. "Is this some sort of home invasion trick, so you can rob us?"

I pulled up my shirt, exposing the bandages. "Do you see this? Fractured rib." I waved my cast under her nose. "Broken wrist." I pointed to my forehead. "Four stitches. Someone is trying to kill me. The hospital released me last night. I'm in no condition to rob anybody." I let go of my shirt, groaning weakly and trying to look pathetic. I knew her weaknesses. That ought to be good for something.

"Oh, dear." Rachel hesitated for two seconds, then knelt beside me. "Let me get a closer look." She carefully cleaned the wound. "Have you had a tetanus shot recently? Here, let's swab it with hydrogen peroxide."

I relaxed for the first time since my ordeal began. "You should be a nurse."

Rachel pulled out a gauze bandage and taped it over the wound. "Yeah, that's what my best friend always told me."

"You really should go to nursing school." Rachel and I had talked about this many, many times, because she didn't know what she wanted to do after graduation. Her parents wanted her to be a lawyer like her dad. "Tell me about your friend."

"She's dead and buried," Rachel said, her eyes watering.

"You mean 'cremated,' don't you?"

Rachel pulled back her hand and frowned at me. "How did you know that?"

"Rachel, do you remember the spring break I couldn't go to Tybee Island with you because I had to finish my economics class report?"

"What?" Rachel's face paled.

"It's me, Lindsey."

"Uh-uh! No, that's impossible." Rachel jumped to her feet and backed away from me.

"No, it's not. Listen to me. You refused to go to the beach without me. After I finished my paper, we sat around, watched chick flicks, and ate popcorn. You said it was more fun than lying on the beach and getting too much sun."

Rachel moved to the red sofa and collapsed on the edge of the cushion. "Who told you that?"

"Remember the evening we were initiated into Beta Club with a scavenger hunt? We decided the best place to get a snake was to break into Johnny Whitmire's bedroom and borrow his pet anaconda. When you boosted me up to the porch roof, you slipped and we landed butt-first into the rose trellis. Remember all those thorns we pulled out of our backsides?"

Rachel slid off the cushion and sank to the floor. "Stop it! This isn't funny!"

My heart thumped wildly in my chest, and I could hear the fear in her voice. I almost had her convinced. "You know who I am, Rachel. Remember the toga party at Freddy Humplemyer's? He pulled off your sheet and left you standing in front of everyone in your red bra and panties. I squirted Freddy and his friends with the fire extinguisher, while you ran out the back door. Did anyone ever find out that you called his parents and told them about the beer at the party?"

Rachel's eyes widened with fright. Shaking her head and breathing heavily, she pushed herself to her feet. "This is insane!"

I stumbled off the sofa. "I let the air out of all four tires on Freddy's truck. And when his parents came home early, they found Freddy and four friends smoking pot."

I reached out to touch Rachel's hand, but she backed away from me until she hit the wall. She stood there frozen, her eyes closed, her breathing fast and shallow, shrieking hysterically. I grabbed her shoulders and shook her hard, but she wouldn't shut up. Not knowing what else to do, I reached out and slapped her across the face. It always worked in the movies. Sure enough, the screaming stopped, replaced by soft whimpering.

I could not believe how she was carrying on. If anyone was entitled to be hysterical, it was me. "Rachel, calm down. Take some deep breaths."

Slowly Rachel's breathing returned to normal and she opened her eyes. "Dr. Anderson was right," she said, swallowing hard.

I gripped her shoulders tightly. "Right about what?"

"Dr. Anderson said some crazy girl who thought she was Lindsey would come to see me. And here you are."

I shook her by the shoulders. "Rachel, I am Lindsey."

"God help us!" A strangled sound escaped from her throat.

"I wish God would help us. I wish I could get my old body back. I wish I could get back my life and my friends. I want to graduate from East Lake High. I want to go to Stanford and play soccer."

Rachel's eyes widened, and her cheeks flushed. "Lindsey? Is it really you?"

CHAPTER SEVENTEEN
DOWN AND OUT

Slowly I guided Rachel over to the comfy sofa. We sat down together, side by side, her eyes never leaving mine. I grabbed her hands and squeezed. "I know this is a big shock."

"Uh-huh." Rachel blinked and gulped.

I wiped a tear off her cheek. "It's totally unbelievable."

Her eyes were still locked on mine. "Uh-huh."

I had known Rachel since kindergarten. This was the first time I had ever seen her at a loss for words. "Can you say anything besides 'uh-huh'?"

"Uh-uh." She slowly lifted a hand to my face and stroked my cheek. "Don't you understand? I was next to you on the field. We were hugging each other and jumping up and down and screaming." She paused. Another tear trickled down her cheek. "You were up on our shoulders and then . . . and then you just . . . fell . . . down. Don't you remember?"

I leaned back into the sofa and closed my eyes. "I remember kicking the ball and making the goal. I remember the screaming and the ground shaking. I remember sitting on your shoulders. Then nothing until I woke up in the hospital a few days ago." I opened my eyes and looked into hers. "In this body that is <u>not</u> mine. Rachel, I am not myself today. I will never be myself, again."

Rachel shook her head. "I don't understand. How is this possible? It's only in the movies that people end up in the wrong bodies."

"Yeah. And in the end, after learning some life lesson, they get their real bodies back."

Rachel sat up straight. "Exactly!" Her shoulders slumped. "But you don't have your real body to get back."

"I know." I swatted Annabeth's fly-a-way hair out of my eyes and sighed. "I'm just a box of ashes."

Rachel nodded. "That's true, Lindsey, but your life simply can't get any worse than that, can it?"

"Rachel, you don't know the half of it." For the next hour I described to her in gory details what had happened to me since the game. How no one believed I was Lindsey. I told her about Neeley, a sex trafficking victim, the Atlanta police detective, and Mike the Motivator. The confrontation between me and Dad. Meeting with the weird psychologist. Being chased and shot at. And, of course, my heated discussions with Justin.

"Justin Hopkins?" Rachel squealed. "Yuck! That disgusting, creepy little worm, who torments you with his childish antics?"

I nodded. "Because he wants me to know he likes me."

Rachel choked. "What? Are you serious? He's gotta be three years younger than you. Is he fifteen yet?" Then she covered her mouth and laughed. "That is so middle school behavior!"

"I know! Get this: He was angry at Annabeth for pretending to be me. Finally, I convinced him I really was Lindsey." As much as I had despised him at East Lake High, I now had to consider Justin an ally. After all, I had so few. Besides, was it his fault he's so smart he had to skip three grades? "He truly wants to help me, Rachel. Maybe I misjudged him."

Rachel grabbed my wrist. "Get out! You can't be serious?!"

"Very serious." Then I told her how I was moved from the hospital for protection, chased by Annabeth's drug-dealing pimp, and screamed at and rejected by my own dad. I explained about the "ghostbusters" from Los Angeles, how Annabeth stole Tony's drug money, and why Tony beat up Neeley and wanted to kill me to get back his money. "Since I've only been in Annabeth's body a few days, how could I possibly know what she did with his money?"

A wide-eyed Rachel sat there with her jaw gaping, listening in silence to every word. "This is like a freaking thriller cop show on TV." She threw her arms around me and hugged me tightly.

For the first time since I woke up in the hospital, I felt safe. And loved. But the feeling only lasted a few seconds. Once the hug was over, it was back to my nightmare reality. "Rachel, I need help getting my life back."

"And how are you going to do that? Your real body is gone. Your new body doesn't look anything like Lindsey. Not even close. Not to mention that Annabeth's body comes with lots and lots of bad juju baggage."

I picked up one of the sofa pillows and smacked her on top of the head. "Shut up! You think I don't know all that?"

Rachel yanked the pillow out of my hands and hit me back. "Then what are you going to do? Do you have a plan?"

I don't know why, but suddenly all I could think about was Scarlett O'Hara in "Gone with the Wind." How she wanted to go back to Tara. Then I knew what I wanted to do. "I want to go to Oakland."

"The cemetery?" Rachel's eyes just about bugged out of their sockets. She slid down to the floor and looked at me like I'd suggested her brother was descended from a Greek god. "Why?"

Yes, Lindsey, why? Probably because of Dad, I figured. When Mom died, I remembered telling him I wanted to be buried next to her. Dad patiently explained that when my time came, my husband would want me buried next to him. But I have no husband, and I've outlived my mom. "I need to go to the cemetery, because that's where my ashes are, right?"

Rachel nodded. "Yes, a private graveside service is scheduled for noon today to inter your ashes. But I don't know a single person who was invited to that."

"What time is it now?" I grabbed Rachel's wrist and looked at her Apple watch, an early graduation present from her parents. "It's 11:30. If we hurry, we can make it."

Rachel pinned me down on the sofa. "Absolutely not, Lindsey! It's a private ceremony for your father and Bishop Hailey."

But, of course, I thought. Bishop John Hailey had presided at my mom's funeral service. A family of scientists, the Andersons had never been regular church goers. Yet Dad and Bishop Hailey were close friends and confidants, and played golf together as often as time permitted. "We could hide behind a tombstone and watch?"

"I said no, Lindsey. I know you. You would confront your father, again, and it would be a disaster. Your dad has asked for privacy. You need to respect that. A memorial service is being planned for family and friends at a later date."

I sighed loudly. "You're right, Rachel, but can we go later today?"

Now it was Rachel's turn to sigh loudly. "I don't understand why you want to go to the cemetery. That sounds creepy. And twisted."

Twisted? To see where they put my remains? I decided not to mention about visiting the morgue. I let my breath out in a loud hiss. "I know how it sounds, but—" Now that I thought about it, if this situation were reversed, and it was Rachel who wanted to go the cemetery to see where her ashes were interred, then perhaps I would think the same thing. "Rachel, it may sound that way to you, but I need to see where my ashes are. I need to know that my body isn't in a morgue refrigerator somewhere. Before I can move on, Rachel, I have to know with certainty that I can never get my body back. Call it closure." Besides, I wanted to visit Mom's grave. I often went there to talk to her. I always felt a sense of peace, afterwards.

"Okay, fine. I'll go, but only on one condition." Rachel pulled herself off the floor.

"What?" Did she want to go in separate cars? Did I need to ride in the trunk?

"You have to change into decent clothes, and do something with your hair. I cannot be seen in public with you looking like that." She sniffed and wrinkled her nose. "Not to mention that you smell bad."

"What's wrong with—" I looked at my image in the mirror by the door. I had forgotten about Annabeth's choice of clothes.

"I would be totally humiliated if someone saw you looking like that."

"Like what, Rachel? A teenage hooker? Go ahead, say it— spit it out." *Holy crap!* I thought we were best friends. I glanced at my reflection one more time. *Be honest, Lindsey, would you leave the house with Rachel, if she looked this bad?*

Rachel hung her head. "I'm sorry. It's just that—well, you know?"

"No, tell me." But I understood. I was having a hard time getting used to Annabeth and Neeley's sordid lives and history myself. What was it that Mom used to whisper whenever we saw homeless people living in cardboard boxes or heard that someone's home burned down or that she knew parents who lost a child to street violence? "But by the grace of God, I am what I am," I whispered.

"What was that?"

"Something my mother used to say about bad things happening to people. I think it meant that it was only by the grace of God that something bad wasn't happening to her."

"Oh." Rachel frowned and nodded. "I get it. So, by the grace of God, I could be the one in Annabeth's body. Or we both could be sex trafficking victims?"

"I think that's exactly it." I was silent for a moment before speaking, again. "And I will definitely clean up my act before being seen in public with you. That was Neeley and Annabeth's plan, too."

"I hope that I didn't offend you, Lindsey, but if your spirit or soul—or whatever—is inside Annabeth's body, wouldn't you want to look and act like—well, you know?"

"Like one of the 'East Lake Bombers'?"

"Exactly." She stepped back, tilted her head and looked at me from head to toe. Then she inhaled a deep breath and sighed loudly. She shook her head. "I hate to tell you this, Lindsey, but your new body is really skinny. I'm guessing a size zero. What do you think?"

For some reason the witch scene from "The Wizard of Oz" flashed through my mind—the one where Dorothy throws the bucket of water on the Wicked Witch, and she slowly and agonizingly shrinks down to nothing. A lump formed in my throat. My beautiful athletic body was gone. I now had a body like one of those waif-like, very thin, teenage models.

Rachel ran over and gave me a hug. I sobbed. She sobbed. It was a good "East Lake Bomber" bonding moment.

"We'll always stick together," Rachel whispered.

But for one brief instance, I thought I saw a look of doubt flash across her face. "Yes, Rachel, together forever."

Together we recited the end of the mantra. "In good times and in bad."

And these were some really, really bad times.

CHAPTER EIGHTEEN
THRIFT HOUSE BARGAINS

The musty smell of old clothes hit me as soon as we opened the Good Sisters' Thrift House door. As the most respected and admired fashionista at East Lake High, Rachel said this was the place to go for decent-looking, cheap clothes that would fit Annabeth's body. Like my own size 10 clothes, Rachel's size 8 outfits were also too big.

Following Rachel up and down the rows of clothes, I watched as she slid hangered dresses, shirts, pants, and skirts up and down the racks. Then she rooted around in stacks and piles of shorts and T-shirts that covered three tables. How many times had she and I traipsed between her house and the Thrift House in hopes of finding a cast-off Christian Dior dress or Oscar de la Renta evening gown, chattering and gossiping along the way as only best friends can?

I was sorting through an assortment of designer leather bags and purses, when Rachel threw me a pair of long pants. Bottega Veneta, according to the label. The original price tag—$490—

was still hanging from the side. In the dressing room, I stripped off Annabeth's clothes, stepped into the long pants and fastened them around my waist.

Rachel looked down at the seat of the pants and shook her head. "Well, scratch that pair. You need more butt to fill it out. Here, try this on." She handed me a like-new Jones of New York floral blouse with three-quarter length sleeves. "I'll be right back."

By the time I had the blouse buttoned up, Rachel was back with a pair of cantaloupe-colored Capri's, which fit Annabeth's body perfectly, and matched the blouse.

"Much better," Rachel said, standing back to admire the combination. "For someone who no longer has any boobs or butt, it's not a bad look." She smirked. "I think I'm willing to be seen in public with you now."

I looked at myself in the mirror and sighed. "I appreciate your help Rachel, but this just isn't me."

"It fits the 'new' outside you perfectly," Rachel pointed out. "You're still the old you on the inside."

Ah, yes, the "new" me on the outside.

Rachel pulled a brush out of her bag and went to work on Annabeth's blah hair. I have to admit that by the time she brushed it back and braided the hair down my back, it wasn't bad. With the addition of a little lip gloss and mascara, Rachel had me looking a few years older than the 14-year-old girl I had become.

One long look in the mirror and I was glad Kevin Atkins and I had broken up. As the state running back star for East Lake, he had accepted a football scholarship to the University of Florida for the fall and wanted me to play soccer there. But the Stanford soccer team was number one in the nation, and I didn't want to play anywhere else. If he could see me now, I felt sure Mr. Senior

Football Star would not want to be seen in public with the new me. I wondered if he cried when he heard I had died?

• • • • •

Once Rachel parked her black Sentra at Oakland Cemetery, a self-imposed silence passed between us. We walked through the brick arch and iron gates into the old Atlanta cemetery, which was founded in 1850. Downtown Atlanta skyscrapers looked down on us, as we made our way past angelic sculpture, family crypts, and huge marble monuments, surrounded by ancient oaks and magnolias. We walked past my favorite statue of the Lion of Atlanta that guarded the graves of 3,000 Confederate soldiers. Then up a gentle slope and down the other side to my mother's grave.

The double granite tombstone bore the name Anderson in all caps. Underneath were the names of my parents, their birth dates, and my mother's death date. Between my mother's gravesite and my dad's future resting place was a small mound of reddish-brown dirt. An 8-inch cube of black stone next to it caught my eye. One long-stemmed white rose lay on top of it. I stooped down to read the small engraved brass plate fastened to the stone:

Lindsey Elise Anderson
2002-2020

I sank to the ground. *Well, Lindsey, you wanted closure. Here it is.* I reached out and ran my fingers over the engraved letters. Tremors ran up my spine. No more hope of ever getting my body back. Tears ran down my cheeks. Here I go again. Just like an old menopausal woman.

Rachel dropped to the ground beside me and put her arm around my shoulders.

I sighed. "This just seems weird."

"How's that?" she asked.

"My ashes are down there, and I'm up here."

"Yeah, that's weird, all right." Rachel bit her lower lip. "Just think, if your father hadn't had you cremated, we could dig up your body and freeze it until we figured out how to get you back inside."

I grunted. "It's a little late now. But before I found out my body was cremated, I asked Dr. Hopkins to help me get my body back. He said he wasn't Dr. Frankenstein."

"Bet he was thinking of decomposition and maggots," Rachel muttered.

Pictures of zombies with sunken eyes and rotting flesh flashed through my mind. "I think bodies are too well-preserved nowadays to have that problem. But it's probably easier to get your body back, if it hasn't been autopsied and embalmed." I turned when I heard strange sounds behind me. Rachel was holding both hands over her mouth. Was she getting ready to hurl?

"When did you find out your body was dead?" Rachel asked, her mouth twisted ever so slightly. Then her face turned red, and her whole body convulsed.

Just as I was convinced that she was choking to death, a strangled giggle erupted. "Rachel, this isn't funny! I'm dead!"

"I know . . . I know . . ." More giggles escaped. "I can't help myself! You sound so serious and clinical—like a doctor."

Then the dam broke, and my so-called BFF burst into hysterical laughter. Honking and snorting, even. I stared at her in disbelief. She had gone berserk because I was dead? Not only dead, but talking to me about it. Matter-of-factly. Then a big guffaw rolled up from my own belly and exploded out of my mouth. "Don't make me laugh." I leaned over and held my sides. "It hurts!"

"I know," Rachel said with a laugh and bent over double. "I'm sorry. Can't stop."

We both laughed until we cried, and Rachel fell over backwards on the grass, rolling from side to side. I can't explain why, but the laughing actually made me feel better. Like the whole world hadn't really fallen on my head. Like maybe my life would be all right after all. But at the moment, I wasn't sure how.

Two elderly women, their arms loaded with flowers, stopped a few feet away. Rachel, wiping her eyes, sat up and tried to look solemn. She pointed at my parents' tombstone. "Our best friend's ashes are buried down there."

I sat up. "A wonderful, kind, caring friend. A great loss."

"We're sorry to hear that," one of the women said. "It's doubly sad when the deceased is so young."

We looked at each other gravely, nodded, and erupted into hysterics.

The two elderly women shook their heads and continued on their way. "Mattie, you never know how some people are going to react to grief," said one of the elderly women, glancing back at us, as we embraced each other and continued to laugh.

Mattie rolled her eyes heavenward. "No, you just never do."

Returning to the car in the cemetery parking area, I felt like the top of my head might come off. My stomach began to cramp. Was it from too much laughing? I gasped and bent over double, leaning on Rachel for support. *Holy crap!* How stupid of me! I had forgotten to take my methadone.

"What's wrong? You okay?" Rachel asked, helping me over to a marble bench. "How can I help?"

"Nothing. No biggie. I'm addicted to heroin, and I didn't make my connection today."

"That's not funny," Rachel said.

"I'm not laughing!" Pain was never funny.

"You don't do drugs," Rachel said.

"No, I don't, but Annabeth did, and this body is going through withdrawal." My voice trailed off as my breath ran out. Beads of sweat popped out on my forehead. "Justin's dad—"

"Dr. Hopkins?"

"Yes, him."

"He treated you at the hospital?" Rachel asked.

I nodded. "He started me on methadone to help with withdrawal."

"Mmm. You know that girl Gillie in our trig class? Didn't she say her cousin sells drugs?" Rachel asked.

I sighed. "It's not a problem," I said. "I have some methadone squirreled away in my backpack."

"Okay then, let's haul it back to my house!"

•   •   •   •   •   •

I lay on Rachel's comfy sofa with a cold, damp cloth on my forehead. The contents of Annabeth's backpack spread out on the coffee table.

"How long before the methadone takes effect?" Rachel asked, wiping my forehead with the cloth.

"Not much longer." Not fast enough to suit me, I thought, wishing Annabeth had been addicted to cigarettes instead. But having never picked up the smoking habit—Dad would have killed me—what did I know?

"How about the rest of your body? Any dressing need changing?" Rachel grasped her hands together and nodded at me.

"Rachel, you're hovering," I said. "You know I hate that." But I'd rather have loving attention than cold rejection any day. I twisted my head to look at Rachel over the washcloth. "It's okay. I know you can't help it. It's your nursing gene." I grimaced and willed the throbbing in the top of my head to go away.

Rachel backed away from the sofa. "Just because I care about you and how you feel, Lindsey Anderson, doesn't mean I need to be a nurse."

"One day you'll realize I'm right." I watched Rachel wander over and start to examine Annabeth's clothes and personal items.

"She certainly didn't have your taste in clothes," Rachel said, holding up a scarlet red bustier.

"She was a 14-year-old sex trafficking victim." I tried not to sound too defensive. "She was young. Didn't you ever look at the sexy apparel in a Frederick's of Hollywood catalog?"

"Maybe in the ninth grade, but I wouldn't be caught dead wearing this stuff. There's a difference between sexy and slutty." Rachel picked up Annabeth's diary. "Hey, what's this?"

I sat up long enough to snatch the diary out of her hand. "That's mine!"

"Well, excuse me! When did you start keeping a journal?"

I could tell by the expression on her face that Rachel was not happy with my behavior, which was unbecoming of a best friend. "Sorry, Rachel. It's Annabeth's personal diary."

"Then it doesn't belong to you, does it?"

"According to Dr. McCracken, the backpack and everything in it belongs to this body. I'm currently occupying this body, therefore it's mine." I frowned at her.

"Do I get to read it or not?" Rachel asked.

I looked at my best friend. She stood there, glaring down at me, hands on hips. Her chin and lower lip jutted out. We had always shared everything—from homework to intimate secrets. So why was I reluctant to share a diary—one that I had not written—with my best friend? If I wanted to continue any kind of relationship with Rachel, I would have to adjust my attitude. I shrugged and handed her the notebook. "Sure, no problem."

The tension in the room eased. Rachel sat down on the red sofa and thumbed through the pages. She browsed through Annabeth's personal effects and picked up the small key. "Is it all right if I touch this?"

"It's just a key of some sorts. It was in the backpack with the rest of her stuff. Does it look important?"

"Looks like a locker key," Rachel said, putting down Annabeth's journal.

"Locker key?" I swung my legs and feet over, and sat up on the sofa.

"Yeah, you know, like in the bus station, maybe?" Rachel examined the key. "Or a train station. Or even a locker in a museum?"

I chewed my lower lip. "What would she have in a locker?" But I already knew. The stolen money—Tony's money. The money he was willing to kill for.

"Maybe the rest of her belongings? Better clothes?" asked Rachel. "Surely she had something decent to wear somewhere?"

"I sort of doubt that," I said. "She fled Ludowici with very few belongings, and apparently did not acquire much more while working for Tony."

"Do they have lockers at the airport?" Rachel asked.

I picked up the diary and gripped it tightly. "She's never been to an airport."

"How do you know that?"

"I read that in her diary. Besides, airports don't have lockers anymore."

"Why not?" Rachel rolled the key around in the palm of her hand.

I couldn't take my eyes off the key. "They're afraid someone might put a bomb in one of them and blow up the airport terminal. Remember, you can't walk off and leave your luggage unattended?"

"Yeah, yeah, yeah. I know," Rachel said. "Okay, then, how about the bus station or the Amtrak station? Or maybe a locker at a bowling alley or a mall? Where else do they have lockers?"

"Disney World?" I frowned. "Although I did hear Neeley mention the bus station. And I read in the diary that Annabeth met Tony there."

"Who's Neeley?"

"Annabeth's friend. They shared a mattress—uh—an apartment." I had to be careful about providing too much information. I didn't want to totally gross Rachel out.

Rachel ran her fingers over the spiked heels. "Annabeth and Neeley both worked for this pimp, Tony?"

I nodded and stood up. "I'll check out the bus station." I started throwing everything into the backpack.

"You can't go alone." Rachel held out her hand like a school crossing guard.

That was all right with me. Safety in numbers. "Fine! You coming with me?" I threw the backpack over my shoulder.

"Count me in." Rachel picked up her red leather Coach bag.

I gave her a hug. "Thank you! You're the best friend a girl could have."

"Let's be honest here. At the moment, I'm the _only_ friend you have," Rachel said.

"Thanks for nothing." But every word she said was true, so I didn't want to alienate her.

"Okay, let's get out of here before someone starts blubbering." Rachel nudged me toward the door.

When she turned the knob, the door burst open, knocking her backwards into me. We fell like dominos, both of us screaming all the way to the floor.

CHAPTER NINETEEN
MONEY AND TROUBLE

A scowling Justin, his arms folded across his chest, stood over us. "What's the matter? Nobody expecting me?"

"Justin?" I couldn't believe he had found me, again. Was it that obvious where I would go next?

"I really surprised you, didn't I?" He reached down and pulled us to our feet. He grabbed my shoulder. "Did it take you long to convince your East Lake Bomber pal about your new identity?"

I pulled away from his grip and shrugged. "We are best friends."

"And you're Justin, the detestable one," Rachel said. "Why don't you turn around and get lost? Sorry we can't stay and chat, but we're on our way out the door."

Justin laughed. "That's really good, Rachel." Then he grabbed my wrist. "Am I detestable to you, too, Lindsey?"

He was too strong for Annabeth's skinny, frail body. He reeled me in like a puny little fish. Soon we were nose to nose. I could feel the heat from his body and count the sprinkling of pale freckles across his nose. And his eyelashes—I never knew they were so long.

"I knew sooner or later you'd show up here," he said, gripping both shoulders. "Why do you keep running off and leaving me? That just pisses me off."

I was feeling guilty, but not quite sure why.

"Is anyone glad to see me?" He took a step back from me. "What's wrong? You didn't think I would come here looking for you?"

I guess I underestimated him. But in a weird way, I was glad he found me. Not sure why.

"How did you know she'd be here?" asked Rachel

"That's all anyone wants to know?" His eyes were locked on mine. "No one wants to know if I or my parents or Dr. Anderson were killed or maimed by that crazy pimp and his buddy?"

"Obviously you aren't dead or dreadfully injured or you wouldn't be here," I replied, as calmly as possible. "I knew as soon as I left the apartment, Tony would be out the door and after me. He wasn't interested in you, your folks, or my dad."

"And what about at my house? You were supposed to wait for me, but you left," Justin said.

"Not that you care, but I was running for my life." A lump formed in my throat. I swallowed hard. How dare he talk to me like that. "Tony and Dante chased me all the way from your home to mine and shot at me. Then when I left my apartment building, they shot at me, and I was almost killed in the parking deck. I'm lucky to be alive." I touched the small bandage on my forehead and stuck out my lower lip. This usually brought me a little sympathy from Dad, but got me nothing from Justin.

Rachel stepped between us. "All right, you two, let's loosen up."

"You're right, I apologize," Justin acquiesced. "It's really silly of me to get upset because she keeps leaving me to get beat up by her sex trafficking, drug-dealing buddies."

"Had you rather I stayed with you and gotten killed?" In other words, Justin, do you care for me or not?

Justin looked down at his shoes. His voice softened. "No, of course not. I'm glad you got away." He reached out and touched my hand. "I'm happy you're alive."

"And I'm sorry they beat you up." I held out my right hand. "Friends?" I asked, not believing that I had asked that. I had not forgotten that this dork once squirted shaving cream hearts all over my car in the school parking lot.

Justin took my hand in his. "Friends."

I thought he held my hand just a little bit too long, but I decided not to protest. I needed all the friends and allies I could get.

Justin leaned back and frowned. "You look different. Um, no, you look better. Um, your hair . . . it's . . . um . . ." He rubbed the back of his neck and looked down at his feet. "I like your hair like that." He looked back up. "Make-up, too? You cleaned up quite well."

Rachel started giggling. I tried to think of a smart-ass comeback, but nothing came to mind. I glared at them and shook my head. The giggling stopped.

Rachel cleared her throat. "How did you know to look here for Lindsey?"

"Simple process of elimination. After she left her dad's place, I figured the next stop would be here. Actually, Dr. Anderson suggested I look here first. Good to know he was right."

The mention of my dad made my stomach hurt. I touched Justin's arm. "I think you should leave now."

"Not until you tell me where you're going," he said, standing between us and the door.

Rachel and I stood in silence and looked at each other, but not at Justin.

"I'm not letting you leave until I know." He crossed his arms across his chest and stared at us defiantly.

I sighed. "If you must know—to the bus station."

Justin frowned. "That's crazy. Have you forgotten about the two lunatics looking for you? The bus station is in their backyard. Why would you go there?"

I held up the key. "Annabeth had this key in her backpack. We think it's a locker key. Whatever is in the locker may give us some answers."

"What's in the locker?" he asked, glancing at the key.

"I'm not sure," I lied, "but it was important enough for Annabeth to keep."

"That's true," he said.

"Tony claims I have something of his. Maybe it's this key," I pointed out.

"Or what's in the locker," Rachel said.

"Okay, you've sold me," Justin said. "Let's go."

"You want to go with us?" I asked.

"I _am_ going with you."

"I don't know, we're going in my car and it's quite small," I said.

"I don't mind squeezing into the back," he offered, avoiding my glaring stare. "After you."

When we reached my Mustang, Justin stood between me and the driver's door. "I just thought of something. Do you have a driver's license?"

"Of course," I snapped.

"I mean a driver's license with <u>your</u> picture on it?"

I opened my mouth to speak, but froze while I thought about this question. Yes, I had my driver's license, but the photo did not look like my new body. Did Annabeth have a driver's license? *Of course not, you idiot! She's only 14.* I grumbled under my breath.

"I didn't think so. I'm driving. Give me the keys!"

"But this is my car!" I sputtered.

"I don't care. Give me the keys!"

"Hold it!" yelled Rachel. "Justin, you're only 15. No way could you have a driver's license either."

Justin shrugged. "I have a learner's permit."

Rachel snatched the keys out of my hand. "I'm the only legal driver in this group. I'm driving." I stomped around to the passenger's side; Justin hopped in the back. The three of us headed downtown in silence.

●　　　●　　　●　　　●　　　●

The Atlanta Greyhound bus station on Forsyth Street was bustling with activity. We stayed close together as we made our way past dozens of panhandlers camped outside the busy terminal. I looked around in shock. I remembered going to the old bus station with my parents when I was a little girl to pick up my Uncle Chester from Indiana. It had been dark and dingy inside with well-worn wooden seats. This bus station was brighter, but lacked character.

Passengers sat around on uncomfortable-looking metal chairs, hugging suitcases and crying children. Many men, women, and children were sitting or lying on the terminal floor with their luggage. Some of them stared at us with interest as we walked through the large open terminal. And the smell was—well—let's just say it was diverse. A mixture of many odors, like sweat, dirty clothes, stale cigarette smoke, a faint hint of urine, old French fries, truck stop bathroom deodorizer, and several unidentifiable I-really-didn't-want-to-know smells.

We had no trouble spotting the lockers—small keyless lockers.

"I don't believe it!" Rachel said. "Whatever happened to lockers with keys?"

"How about the Amtrak train station?" I asked, trying to avoid a toddler who was slowly smashing the remnants of a chocolate doughnut into her mouth. She smiled at me and reached out to grab my pants leg.

"Before we drive all the way over there, let's call." Justin pulled out his cell phone and headed into a corner, away from the noise. He returned in less than two minutes.

"Well?" asked Rachel.

"No such luck." He popped his cell phone back into his pocket.

"What?" I exclaimed, shooing the sticky-fingered child in the direction of her mother and another doughnut.

"They discontinued their lockers, but they will be glad to store your bags for a price."

"Bummer!" Rachel blurted out.

"Now what?" I asked.

Justin reached for the key. "Let me see it." He examined it closely. "What does NFC stand for?"

Rachel and I looked at the key.

"Could it be a bank?" asked Rachel.

"No," answered Justin. "Safety deposit keys do not look like this."

"They have lockers at Six Flags," I said. "And White Water, too."

Justin gave me his boy-are-you-dumb look. "Yeah, and NFC stands for Not For Chewing."

"You've always been a smartass, haven't you?" Rachel said with a hiss.

I sighed. "This isn't helping. How about a bowling alley or a health club or the Y?"

"Not a bowling alley," mumbled Justin. His eyes narrowed. "A health club might be a possibility. Let's check something." We followed him back to the corner and waited while he Googled Atlanta health clubs. "Wait, I think we have something. Look right here. Nocentini's Fitness Center in Midtown."

"It's worth a try." Rachel didn't sound too enthused.

I grabbed her arm. "If we don't check it out, we'll never know."

"We could drive there, check it out, and still not know," she replied.

I placed my arm around Rachel's shoulders. "Yes, but at least we will have tried."

Nocentini's parking lot was full when Justin pulled in. Mostly newer high-end model cars. BMWs, Mercedes, Lexus, and Cadillacs. No SUVs or mini-vans or old-model cars. This fitness center was definitely not for folks on a tight budget. Just as we were considering double-parking, two female twenty-somethings, glistening and sweaty from their workouts, crawled into a metallic green PT Cruiser and gave up their space.

As we left the Mustang and walked toward the entrance, I noticed a broad-shouldered, thick-necked man in a Hawks T-shirt sitting in a black Ford Escort. Somehow, I couldn't picture him sweating it out on a treadmill or doing dance aerobics. When we walked in front of his car, he looked up from the Atlanta newspaper in his hands. Was it only my imagination or did he seem unusually interested in our arrival?

"Do we have a plan?" Rachel asked, as we approached the front door to the fitness center—a plain, one-story beige brick building with no windows.

"No, we'll wing it," replied Justin, holding open the door. "Just back me up."

The reception area was light and airy with floor to ceiling windows. Black leather sofas faced each other across a glass table covered with the latest issues of *Sports Illustrated, Adventure Kayak, Field and Stream,* and *Mountain Biking.* Pots of palm trees and ficus plants provided a tropical feel.

A tall, young man in his late twenties grinned at us from behind a mahogany counter. "Good afternoon!" he greeted us with a booming bass voice. "Is this your first visit to Nocentini's?"

Justin reached out and shook the man's hand. "Yes, it is. We've heard a lot of good things about this place and just wanted to check it out. For graduation, my Aunt Erma wants to give me a membership to the health club of my choice. I'm Justin Hopkins and these are my friends Rachel and—?" Justin looked at me and blinked.

I stepped forward and shook his hand. "Just call me Lindsey." I avoided Justin's eyes.

"That's great! I'm Dusty and I'm glad you're here. You're gonna love this place!" Dusty looked Rachel over carefully and winked. His biceps strained against the cloth in his too-tight red T-shirt. He turned his attention back to Justin and picked up the phone receiver. "Let me see if I can get someone up front to give you folks a five-dollar tour." He flashed his broad smile, again, and dialed an extension number. "Bambi, could you come up front? We have some prospects waiting for a tour of the facilities."

Dusty hung up and in less than 30 seconds, the door behind him burst open, and a perky blonde girl with a perfect body rushed out, eager and nearly breathless. "Hello, hello," she greeted us, exposing a mouthful of gorgeous professionally-whitened teeth in a luscious smile.

"Bambi, this is Justin, Rachel, and Lindsey. They've heard a lot of good things about the center."

"Great! That makes my job easier!" Bambi looked at me and her forehead wrinkled just the slightest. "Do I know you?"

"No, I don't think so." I shook my head. At least I hoped she didn't. No way could Annabeth afford membership in this club.

Bambi frowned. "You haven't been here before?"

"No, this is my first visit." I smiled agreeably.

"I guess you just remind me of someone else." She shrugged. "Okay, why don't you come right this way, please?"

She opened the door, and we followed her down a wide, long corridor, with doors on both sides. Bambi bounced down the hallway, her very ample bosom jiggling with every step. "First, we'll visit the equipment room."

Rachel and I trailed after Bambi and Justin, until we passed a door marked "Women's Locker Room." I halted and grabbed Rachel's arm. "Excuse me, Bambi, but are the restrooms in here?"

"Yes, but I was saving the locker rooms until the end of the tour." She flashed those whiter-than-white teeth.

"I'll just be miserable if I have to wait." I crushed my thighs together and danced.

"Well, I guess we can wait out here for you," Bambi mumbled. I could tell she wasn't exactly thrilled at the prospect.

Justin started down the corridor. "Wait on her? You gotta be kidding! Come on Bambi, I'm the one you need to sell this fitness center to. This is my graduation present from my aunt." Justin's eyes darted back at me. "It doesn't matter what my friends think. This is my present and my decision."

"Oh! Well, in that case, Justin . . ." Bambi led him down the corridor and into the door marked "Equipment Room" without a backward glance at us.

"Bye," I said with a wave. "We'll catch up with you in a few."

Rachel found locker 252 first. "Here it is! Where's the key?"

Key in hand, I eagerly reached up to insert it in the lock, but found a key was already there. "Unbelievable!"

Rachel stood there dumbfounded. "I don't understand. It says 252 and NFC."

I examined the key in my hand and the other keys in the lockers. "Look closer, Rachel. See the little bit of plastic on the end of this key?"

"Yeah, it's blue. So?"

"All the other keys in here are red. There must be more lockers somewhere else."

We looked at each other expectantly. "The men's room!" we shouted. "Yes!"

We left the women's area and walked casually down the corridor to the door marked "Men's Locker Room." I was almost giddy with anticipation and excitement. No one else was in sight.

Cautiously, we pushed open the door a crack and peeked in. "I don't see anybody." I slipped in, followed closely by Rachel. "Remember, if someone catches us, we're visitors looking for our tour group."

Rachel snorted. "Right!"

I pointed out that the keys in the men's lockers had the blue plastic on the end. I headed to the side and started moving up the left row. A long bench between the lockers was covered with smelly tennis shoes, socks, damp swim suits, and undergarments.

Rachel gagged behind me. "Disgusting! Do all men's locker rooms smell this bad?"

"Probably. They're guys, aren't they? Wait, we're getting close! Over here!" I held my breath, inserted the key and twisted. The door opened. Inside was a medium-sized black leather, zippered duffle bag with two handles on top.

"Open it! Open it!" Rachel said.

"Calm down." I slid the bag forward and stumbled backwards into Rachel. It was heavier than it looked. I lost my grip on the bag and dropped it with a thud to the floor. I could feel my heart rate quicken. I unzipped it and gasped at the sight of thousands of bills: mostly one-hundred-dollar bills. A small black notebook lay on top.

Rachel plunged her hands into the bag and began examining the packet of bills. She squealed, "I've never seen so much cash. Is it real?"

I zipped shut the bag. "Shhh. Calm down. This has to be what those guys are after."

"But where'd all that money come from?" asked Rachel as we headed for the locker room door.

"Drugs would be my guess." I shifted the bag to my other hand. It had to weigh close to 30 pounds. I work out with 10-pound weights at home. This bag definitely weighed more than 20 pounds.

"Annabeth was a pusher?" Rachel asked, pushing open the door. "She was only 14."

"I don't think so. A user definitely. A pusher, no. But her pimp must be, obviously."

"But why would she steal his money?" Rachel asked. "Surely she knew he'd kill her?"

I remembered what Annabeth had written in her diary about Tony. "She hated him, and she was desperate to get away from him."

We exited the men's locker room just as Justin and Bambi walked through the door marked "Exercise Room." I moved next to Rachel and hid the bag behind us. I hoped Bambi didn't see the door close behind us.

"Did you check out the women's facilities?" asked Bambi with a frown.

"We certainly did. And we were very impressed. Right, Rachel?"

"Oh, yes, we were very, very impressed."

We both attempted big, innocent smiles.

Justin sidestepped over and casually glanced behind me. "Is that what I think it is?" he whispered in my ear.

I nodded. "Later."

Justin thanked Bambi for the grand tour. "My pleasure," she replied, shaking his hand and holding it just a tad too long. "If you like, Dustin will talk to you about membership and financing. I'll get back to work. You come back real, soon. Ya'll hear?"

"I can't wait! It's been a pleasure." Justin placed his hand on the door to the lobby, but didn't open it. He waited until Bambi had disappeared through a door marked "Office" at the end of the corridor. Then he turned to me. "Well?"

"It's crammed full of money," I whispered excitedly.

"Thousands of bills!" squealed Rachel. "Maybe a million dollars! What should we do with it?"

"Let's get out of here and discuss it." Justin pushed open the door to the lobby, and the smile on his face evaporated. Annabeth's pimp Tony was standing in the center of the lobby with a revolver pointed at Justin's head. Just like in a TV crime show. Looking like a modern-day Goliath, Dusty lay gagged and pinned to the floor by Dante.

"Why don't we discuss it right now?" Tony grinned viciously, motioning Justin into the lobby. "On second thought, why don't we just have my number one whore hand me my money?"

CHAPTER TWENTY
CONFRONTATION

Hands in the air, Justin walked toward Tony, staying between him and us. I took back every mean thought I'd ever had about Justin. Hoping for some form of help to arrive, I looked to see if some kick-ass guy was headed this way from the parking lot. Someone tough and scary like Dwayne Johnson or Dave Bautista. Even a young version of Arnold Schwarzenegger. But no, poor Justin was on his own.

With his gun on Justin, Tony maneuvered closer to me and his bag of money. Unnoticed, Justin placed his foot in front of Tony, whose eyes were focused on the bag. When Tony stepped on his foot, Justin bent over and screamed, "Ow! My foot!"

Caught off guard, Tony reeled in surprise. Immediately, Justin straightened up and rammed the pimp in the stomach with his head—sending Tony tumbling backwards on top of Dante and Dusty. The revolver slipped from Dante's hand, hit the floor, and fired.

"RUN!" Justin screamed, and chaos broke loose.

Like the girl in the horror movie, I was riveted to the spot, unable to move. Fortunately, Rachel yanked me and the black bag back through the door and down the corridor. Before the door closed behind me, I caught a glimpse of Justin crashing to the floor. Had he been shot? I hesitated, but Rachel grabbed my arm and urged me forward, screaming as we ran, "Help! Police! Fire!" Immediately, two sweating hunks stepped out of the equipment room, and Bambi burst out of her office.

"Bambi, call 911," Rachel screamed. "You're being robbed!"

Gun fire, loud crashing sounds, and shouting could be heard coming from the lobby. Bambi gasped, and her eyes widened. "It's you, again!" She pointed her finger at me. "You're the one who caused all the trouble here last week!"

I cringed. There was no telling how much trouble this body had gotten into. I only hoped Annabeth hadn't murdered anyone or robbed a bank, while I wasn't around. My stomach turned queasy at the thought. If I were arrested for any crimes she had committed, how could I defend myself?

Suddenly behind us, Dusty erupted through the lobby door. His hands and ankles still bound, he hopped and stumbled down the hallway screaming. Dusty's face had turned a purplish red from his efforts.

Not waiting another second, Rachel and I pushed through the double doors that led to an Olympic-size pool. The heat and humidity hit me like a brick wall. Sweat broke out on my face, and the acrid stench of chlorine burned my eyes, causing tears to run down my cheeks. At the far end of the pool we could see the bright red lights of our salvation: EXIT.

One lifeguard stood at attention by his seat. "What's going on?"

"It's awful!" I yelled, not slowing down. "People are shooting each other."

Rachel loped along beside me. "Active shooter in the building! Get out while you can."

We bolted past two matronly, white-haired women, who were toweling off after their swim. Strange, but they both looked familiar to me.

"Mattie, those girls . . ." mumbled the taller one.

"Run for your lives!" Rachel yelled back over her shoulder.

"Didn't we see them at the cemetery, Sara?" Mattie pulled off her white bathing cap and flung her towel around her neck.

Well, if they didn't think we were completely wacky at the cemetery, they certainly will know it now, I thought. We quickly exited through the outside door. Even though we heard women screaming behind us, we didn't stop.

Outside of the rear of the fitness center, we ducked through several backyards and alleys, making our way towards West Peachtree Street. I was leading the way, with Rachel behind me. The bag, which I was clutching against my chest, was getting heavier and my upper body—especially my fractured wrist and ribs—was hurting from the physical exertion.

"Where are we going?" Rachel gasped.

"Away from Tony," I gasped back.

At the intersection of West Peachtree and 14th, I dropped the heavy bag of money and leaned against a light pole. Rubbing my aching shoulders, I tried to catch my breath. "We're not that far from a MARTA station."

Rachel slumped beside me, breathing hard. "Train works for me," she said.

Shouts sounded behind us. I turned and spotted Tony and Dante about a block away, running down the sidewalk in our direction. My heart dropped and my knees felt rubbery. "Let's get out of here," I yelled.

We stepped out into the middle of 14th Street with horns honking, brakes squealing, and drivers cursing while swerving to avoid hitting us. When we reached the far curb safely, I heard a loud "pop" and felt something whiz past my face. Two well-dressed women waiting on the corner for the light to change screamed and dropped to the sidewalk.

I couldn't believe someone would shoot at us in broad daylight on a busy street. "Stay down!" I warned Rachel. As I struggled with my grip on the money bag, I wished that Tony had purchased a bag with wheels. It would have made it easier to steal. Crouching down, my adrenaline pumping, I led Rachel past an office building and headed toward the entrance of the Midtown MARTA Station.

The gray concrete entrance to the station seemed a godsend. Struggling with the heavy bag, I elbowed a hefty brunette in a red dress out of our way and knocked a briefcase from the grasp of some older lawyer type. My heart pounded in my ears. My lungs ached from heavy-duty breathing. The entrance was still 30 feet away, when I heard a woman scream and turned to see Tony and Dante galloping toward us.

"Run!" screamed Rachel.

"I'm too old for this," I gasped, falling behind her.

"Shut up," panted Rachel. "You have the youngest body here. Get moving!"

My 14-year-old body may have been the youngest, but it was way out of shape and still recovering from serious injury. "*Holy crap*," I cried, as we reached the turnstiles. "Do you have a Breeze card?" We were doomed. Cornered like rats by rabid cats.

"Lindsey, you're an idiot!" Rachel scrambled over the top of the turnstile, nearly knocking down two old women trying to use their Breeze cards.

Following my best friend, I pushed aside the gaping-mouth women, slid the bag under, and cleared the turnstile like a high school track star. "I've always wanted to do that!" I explained to the women.

"Hmph!" grunted one of the women. "Young people have no respect for their elders these days."

We sprinted down the escalator and hit the platform running. A north-bound train waited with its doors open.

As I jumped inside the closest car, I saw Tony and Dante at the top of the escalator. "Here they come," I hissed. "Get down!"

"Why won't these stupid doors close?" asked Rachel, as we crouched in the floor, watching Tony and Dante shoving unwary MARTA riders aside on the escalator.

A young man wearing a backpack and AirPod Pro headphones was standing on the opposite end of the car, tapping his foot to music only he could hear. He noticed us crawling in his direction and frowned. "Are ya'll all right?"

"Sure, we just like to crawl around train floors," retorted Rachel, twisting her mouth. She nodded her head in the direction of the platform. "See those two huge guys who just knocked over the little boy?"

The young man looked up and nodded.

"They're trying to kill us!" Rachel said.

While the remaining half a dozen passengers in the car ignored us, this young man—most likely a college student—turned around and reached for the emergency phone.

"This way," I said, tugging on Rachel's sleeve and duck-walking to the connecting train door. I reached up and grabbed the handle. "Holy crap! You know how in the movies the heroine runs from the back to the front of the train through the connecting doors?"

"Yeah, let's go," Rachel said

"They're locked. You can only use them in an emergency."

"What'll we do?" she asked.

"Follow my lead." Staying as close to the train floor as possible, we waited until Tony and Dante burst through the doors at the front of the car. Then we exited by the rear doors. Hunching over, we entered the doors of a car further down the platform. When Tony and Dante followed us, we crept out of the rear set of doors and hid behind a concrete pillar on the platform. Finally, the alarm sounded, the train doors shut, and the train moved out of the station.

We huddled together, embracing the black bag. "Did it work?" Rachel asked.

"I think so," I said, just seconds before Tony grabbed my hair and pulled me to my feet. My eyes teared from the pain. I grabbed his massive steel-trap hands, but couldn't loosen his grip.

"Would you care to repeat that, my sweet, little Magnolia?" he asked.

"Help! Somebody please help me!" I cried out to a middle-aged man in suit and tie, carrying a briefcase, but he turned away and hurried toward the edge of the platform.

Tony released my hair, but his fingers dug into my shoulder. "Shut up! Nobody's gonna help you!"

I sobbed loudly as two well-dressed women walked by. Were they blind? Couldn't they see I was in trouble and needed help?

Rachel tried to crawl away with the money bag, but Dante seized her wrist and twisted it. "Can I kill her now, boss?"

"No, fool!"

Rachel sprung to her feet, soccer-kicked Dante in the groin, and swung the bag by the handle like an Olympic hammer throw—slamming into his shoulder. As his body twisted from the force of the blow, she kicked him in the rear, sending him face down on the concrete. Freed from his grasp, Rachel grabbed the bag and dragged it down the platform, which was filling up with MARTA riders waiting for the next train.

Scowling at the sight of his departing money bag, Tony shoved the muzzle of his revolver under my chin with such force, I nearly blacked out. "Throw me my money or she's dead," he screamed at Rachel and fired a warning shot in the air.

My whole body turned icy. I was fixing to get killed for the second time. And no one—least of all Dad—would care because to them I was already dead and cremated.

MARTA riders waiting on the platform for their train began screaming and running for cover. Rachel halted and turned, her eyes wide with fear. Out of the corner of my eye, I saw Dante on the ground, writhing in pain. But beyond him, I saw the cavalry arriving. Lt. Richards, Dr. Hopkins, Justin, and half a dozen policemen, guns in hand, were cautiously descending the escalators to the train platform. Two policemen hurried towards Dante with weapons drawn.

"Rachel!" I screamed. "Run!"

Tony wrapped his arm around my throat. "Listen up. I'm counting to three. One . . ."

Trying to ignore the fact that I could barely breathe, I considered my options. In the distance, I heard the sound of an approaching train. I saw policemen crouched at the bottom of the escalator, weapons drawn and ready. Lt. Richards was physically restraining Justin. Tony seemed oblivious to everything—except Rachel and his bag of money.

"Two . . ."

Rachel hesitated only briefly before hammer-throwing the money bag toward Tony and the oncoming train. Then life seemed to move in slow motion. I saw Tony's hands reaching up for his money bag. When the bag barely brushed his fingertips, Tony's entire body lunged upward. At the same time, Justin broke away from the policeman and threw himself in my direction, pulling me from Tony's grip. Justin and I rolled away from Tony, the money bag sailed in front of the braking train, and Tony landed face down on the concrete, his head barely stopping on the edge of the platform.

A loud thud and a whump sounded on the tracks below, followed by an explosion of U.S. currency in all denominations. The bills flew through the air and floated down to the tracks and platform. MARTA passengers exiting the train went wild. Scrambling to grab their share of the loot, they tripped over and stepped on a screaming Tony.

While Atlanta's finest rolled over and cuffed a bloody-faced Tony, Justin sat on the concrete platform, holding me tightly in his arms. I sobbed quietly into his chest. Relief surged throughout my body. I might not be myself today, but I was alive, breathing, and safe for the moment.

"You're not doing so bad for a know-it-all 14-year-old," he said.

I pulled back from him. "For an obnoxious little dork, you're not doing too badly either. But couldn't you have gotten here faster? I was nearly killed." I felt my bottom lip start to quiver.

Justin hugged me tighter. "You young girls are all alike—never satisfied, not even when someone saves your life."

Rachel plopped down on the platform next to us and gave me a hug. We watched as Dante and a sullen Tony were hauled up the escalator. A swarm of policemen were left with the seemingly impossible task of collecting the scattered money and bringing order to the MARTA station.

Lt. Richards approached our tiny island of calm in a chaotic sea. "Everyone okay here?"

"Just scared half to death," replied Rachel.

The detective nodded. "That's understandable when you find yourself on the wrong end of a revolver." He extended his hand to Rachel and pulled her to her feet.

As Justin helped me up, the detective grabbed his shoulder. "Justin, you and your friends need to come to the station to answer a few questions. I certainly hope you have lots of answers."

Justin tightened his arm around me. "So do I, sir, so do I."

CHAPTER TWENTY-ONE
PICKING UP THE PIECES

Rachel, Justin, and I sat around a gray, metal table in an interview room at the Midtown Atlanta Police Precinct. I was relieved to see that this room did not have a large mirror on the concrete wall with who-knows-who watching our every move. Of course, the room was probably bugged, but I decided not to think about that.

I had a headache developing behind my right eye, my body ached all over, and I was completely exhausted. I only wanted to crawl in a hole and sleep for a month. I felt dirty and stinky from sweat. How long had it been since I last showered? I was ready to get out of here. Unfortunately, Lt. Richards was not finished with us. I yawned big and made no attempt to conceal it. Would he take the hint? Was he hoping if he wore us down a little bit more, we would confess to all of his unsolved cases?

Lt. Richards—his baggy coat removed, sleeves rolled up, and no crushed fedora in sight—paced back and forth across the windowless room. Occasionally he would remove a small notepad from his pocket and scribble something. After a few moments of silence, he halted across the table from us. "Tell me if I understand this correctly. You—" He pointed at Rachel with his pencil. "—do not know Miss Shepard here." He nodded his head toward me.

"That's right," Rachel said, suddenly taking an unusual interest in a wart on her thumb.

Did that make her look suspicious? I glanced at Lt. Richards, but he didn't blink.

"She and Justin arrived at the fitness center the same time I did," she added.

"I see." He paused; his eyes narrowed. "But you were a friend of Lindsey Anderson?"

Rachel nodded. "Yes, we were best friends. We both played soccer for East Lake High."

Trying not to squirm, I quickly shot a glance at Justin, who was seriously studying long scratches on the table top. I wanted to shriek out that I was Lindsey Anderson trapped in Annabeth's body, but Justin and Rachel said it was a bad idea. But was telling a lie to a cop ever a good idea?

"What a coincidence," Lt. Richards said.

A knock sounded, and the interview room door opened. A policeman entered with Dr. Hopkins.

Justin jumped up. "Dad?"

"What's going on?" Dr. Hopkins asked.

I opened my mouth to answer, but Justin frowned and shook his head in my direction. He looked at his dad and slid forward to the edge of his seat.

"Just tying up some loose ends, Dr. Hopkins." Lt. Richards pointed to an empty chair. "Care to join us?"

"Is there a problem?" Dr. Hopkins asked, sitting down. He didn't look happy. "Didn't you capture the men who tried to kill Annabeth Shephard and Neeley Hill?"

I held my breath.

Lt. Richards looked straight at me. "Yes. They were the same men who nearly killed the night security guard at the building where Miss Anderson lived with her father. The same men who critically wounded the driver of a bus on which Miss Shephard was a passenger. And—" he paused, "—the same men who assaulted an Atlanta police officer."

My cheeks began to feel warm.

The detective turned back to Dr. Hopkins. "What is the connection between Miss Shephard and the late Lindsey Anderson?"

"I'm not sure I understand, detective," replied Dr. Hopkins. "They were both admitted to St. Mary's ER at the same time, but that's the only connection I know."

"I don't believe in coincidences." Lt. Richards placed his hands on the table and leaned toward me. "When I first interviewed Miss Shephard in the hospital, she was convinced she'd been playing in a soccer game—just like Miss Anderson."

"I told you, Miss Shephard had just regained consciousness. She was confused," Dr. Hopkins explained.

"Yeah, that's exactly the same story I got from Dr. McCracken." Lt. Richards looked at Rachel, Justin, and me. "The staff at the fitness center said the three of them—" He waved his hand at us. "—arrived together." Rachel opened her mouth to speak, but Lt. Richards held up his hand. "I'm not finished. And now we have a St. Mary's psychologist who was severely beaten on Metropolitan Parkway by this Dante fellow and friends."

Dr. Hopkins' face turned pale. "Bill Epting?"

Bill Epting? I swallowed hard. The doctor who talked to me in the hospital? The one Dr. McCracken said was bringing the "ghostbusters" to town?

Lt. Richards smiled. "Ah, so you know Dr. Epting?"

"Of course, I know him. What was he doing on Metropolitan Parkway?" Dr. Hopkins asked, leaning forward.

Lt. Richards sat on the edge of the table and examined his fingertips. "Funny you should ask. It's an interesting story he shared with me. Since he's suffering from a serious concussion, I'm not sure how much of his story—if any of it—I can believe. He seems to think that Miss Anderson is occupying Miss Shephard's body."

Dr. Hopkins fell back into his seat. Rachel closed her eyes. Justin grabbed my hand. My stomach lurched. I knew we should have told the truth. Would we all go to jail now? No, not me. They'd send me to a lab in some federal research facility. Probably where they keep all those aliens that crash land on Earth.

"Oh, it gets better." Lt. Richards rubbed his hands together. "He says some parapsychologists flew out from Los Angeles to meet Miss Shephard, a.k.a. Miss Anderson, but she apparently had checked out of the hospital. Is that funny or what?"

"You know she left the hospital because her pimp was trying to kill her," Dr. Hopkins protested. "Your man was on the street guarding her."

"That's right!" Lt. Richards jumped off the table and approached Dr. Hopkins. "And he almost got killed for it, too!"

Justin's dad glared at the detective.

Lt. Richards turned around and paced to the other end of the table. He turned, again, arms crossed. "Dr. Epting told me he asked where he could find Miss Shephard. He said you told him to go down to Metropolitan Parkway and check with her pimp."

Dr. Hopkins grimaced. "I wasn't serious."

"Too bad for poor Dr. Epting, because he believed you and was nearly killed for his troubles."

Dr. Hopkins jumped to his feet. "Look, detective, you have two murderers, drug dealers, and sex traffickers behind bars, a list of names that will lead to other arrests, plus a bag of drug and prostitution money."

Lt. Richards scowled.

"Or as much as you could recover from the train tracks and—uh—other witnesses at the station. Also, Miss Shephard has agreed to testify in court against the two men. We've told you everything we know. Can we go now?"

I nodded my head in agreement. I couldn't have said it better. If I didn't get out of this room, I was going to hurl all over everyone.

"I guess—for now." Lt. Richards opened the door. Rachel, Justin, and Dr. Hopkins walked out, but when I tried to leave, the detective grabbed my arm. "One moment, Miss Shephard—or whoever you are." He glared at me. "Something's not right here. You know it, and I know it. Eventually I'll figure it out, then we'll talk, again." He loosened his grip.

I walked past him and out the door. He was correct, something wasn't right, but if I were lucky, he wouldn't ever figure it out.

·　　　·　　　·　　　·

Dr. Hopkins offered to drive Rachel and me back to her house. I didn't protest. "I'm very glad Tony and Dante are out of your life," he said, glancing at me in his rearview mirror.

"Not half as glad as I am," I replied from my seat next to Rachel. "But I still have to testify at their trial."

"We'll deal with that when the time comes," Dr. Hopkins said. "In the meantime, you need to think about the rest of your life."

"The rest of _my_ life? Or the rest of <u>this</u> life?" I asked.

"I know you don't want to hear this, but I don't think there's anyway you can pick up the pieces of Lindsey's life and move on," said Rachel, who was sitting on my right.

"You're saying you want me to stay a teenage hooker?" My voice cracked with emotion at the thought. Even if I were starving to death, I didn't think I could sell my body. "Or were you talking about me becoming a foster child?" I pictured me in a group home, wearing baggy, hand-me-down dresses, and carrying around my possessions in a black trash bag. "My options are sort of limited, in case you hadn't noticed."

"That's not what I meant," She said, rubbing my shoulder. "No one is going to accept you as Lindsey Anderson. No one will believe your story. They'll lock you up in the psycho ward forever."

"She has a point," Justin said from the front passenger seat. "They'll drug you and make you talk to a psychiatrist every day."

I had visions of me in a striped bathrobe, sitting in a large day room, drool running out of the corner of my mouth. We sat in silence for a few minutes, staring out of the car windows.

Rachel clasped my hand. "No matter what you decide to do, Lindsey, we'll always be best friends."

Always best friends? "Rachel, you're fixing to graduate and head off to college." *Holy crap*, there went the lump in my throat, again.

Rachel gave me a hug. "Lindsey, I'll always stay in touch with you. Wherever you are—an orphanage, a foster home, a sleazy motel—"

I hit her in the side with my elbow. "That's not funny, Rachel."

"Ouch! That hurt! I was only trying to lighten things up."

Justin turned around in his seat. "That's not helping."

"I have some news, Lindsey," Dr. Hopkins said. "Your high school is awarding your diploma posthumously, and your dad will be there to accept it himself."

My eyes stung and filled with tears. "I have to go to graduation."

"Do you think that's a good idea?" Justin asked.

"I want to see Rachel graduate," I said, my lower lip sliding out into a pout. "And I'm going to the graduation party afterwards, too."

"But that's only for graduates and family members," Rachel said.

"Then I will be your cousin from Canada. Will my dad be there?"

"He's invited," Dr. Hopkins said. "The school will present a special plaque to him."

"And the Letter Club has created a special athletic scholarship in your memory," Rachel said. "They've already collected more than $18,000."

"See? Lots of folks love and miss Lindsey Anderson," Justin said.

Not as much as I do.

CHAPTER TWENTY-TWO
LUDOWICI

Rachel's mom, Alison Adams, was a member of Junior League of East Lake, a group of community women dedicated to improving the social and economic conditions of others. The group did a lot of work with underprivileged children. Once Dr. Hopkins and Dr. McCracken explained that I needed a temporary place to stay until I was assigned a home in the foster care system, Rachel's parents agreed that I could stay with them and be mentored by Rachel.

As soon as I heard the news, I started thinking about going to Ludowici. The South Georgia town had been in the back of my mind since I read about it in Annabeth's diary. Here was where this body had its roots, where Annabeth was born and grew up, and where I had to go before I could make any decisions about the rest of my life.

On Wikipedia, I learned Ludowici is a small South Georgia town with one stop light, a few churches, three public schools, one small grocery store, a Dollar General, a Subway, Dairy

Queen, Huddle House, and a couple of restaurants. One of those small rural towns that teenagers flee after high school graduation and never return.

I thought more about Ludowici while eating a meat loaf dinner at Rachel's house. Her mom served it with buttery mashed potatoes, green beans, and what my dad called cooked-to-death yellow squash. I could smell dessert—brown sugar, apples and cinnamon—long before the apple pie showed up on the table. Generous slices were cut and topped with a scoop of vanilla bean ice cream. It was lip-smacking good.

After we finished dessert and helped with the dishes, Rachel and I stretched out on her sleigh bed and relaxed. We were too stuffed to do anything else. Rachel's thick, gold and burgundy comforter felt good under my back. With the future of a foster home looming on my horizon, I was grateful that I could stay at Rachel's home for a few more days. Her mother seemed happy that Rachel had a new best friend and wasn't moping about the house. If only she knew the real truth.

Sinking my head into one of the matching shams, I ran fingers through my hair, still damp and squeaky clean from a pre-dinner shower. It was time to share my decision with my best friend. "How about a road trip tomorrow? Two women, my Mustang convertible, the open road—"

Rachel rolled over on her side and looked at me. "A road trip? Where?"

"Ludowici."

Grabbing a pillow, Rachel threw it at me. "Get serious!" She sat up on her knees and looked at me strangely. Like I'd said I wanted to go sky diving. Then her jaw dropped. "Omigosh! You are serious!"

I threw the pillow back at her. "Yes, I really want to go."

"But Ludowici is a four-hour drive from here!" she said. "That's not a road trip, Lindsey—that's an adventure."

"I seem to remember a weekend once when you dragged me on a road trip to New Orleans," I said, raising my right eyebrow. "Correct me if I'm wrong, but isn't that slightly more than a four-hour drive? I bet your parents still don't know where we went."

Rachel's face turned pink. She tugged on the hem of her Daisy Duck night shirt and rubbed the back of her head. "Why Ludowici?"

"Annabeth came from there."

"So?"

I hated it when she plied me with questions I didn't want to answer. "Rachel, this body is from there."

Rachel wiggled off the bed and looked down at me. "I still don't understand."

I reached out, grabbed Rachel's hand and pulled her back down on the bed. "I know you don't understand, but I need to go there. I have to see Annabeth's past—her hometown, her high school, and the farm where she was raised."

Rachel pulled back her hand. "Is this like going to the cemetery? You need this for closure?"

I shook my head. "No, I need to do this for some fact gathering."

Rachel put her chin on my shoulder. "This might not be such a good idea. What if Annabeth's friends see you?"

"If that happens, I'll deal with it."

She leaned over into my face. "What about her mother? Surely you don't want to see her?"

I sighed. "Maybe . . ."

Rachel gasped. "You can't be serious?"

"I don't know. I'm just not sure yet."

"And what about her stepfather?" Rachel asked.

"Then I'll have him arrested." Or kill him. At the very least, I'd kick him where I knew it would hurt.

I hugged Rachel. "Well, what do you say? Are you going with me or not?"

"This is that important to you?"

I nodded. This was absolutely necessary. To me, going to Ludowici and examining the pieces of Annabeth's life was like being an adopted child and wanting to know about the parents who gave you up for adoption, and if you had any brothers or sisters or any bad genes. It just made perfect sense to me.

She sighed. Her shoulders sagged. "Well, since you went with me to New Orleans, I guess I can go with you to Ludowici," Rachel said. "We're the East Lake Bombers and we have to stick together."

I jumped on the bed. "Thanks! You're absolutely my very favorite best friend."

Rachel smirked. "Yeah, don't know of anybody else who'd give a dead best friend the time of day."

"Oh, Rachel, that is soooooo bad!" I gave her a playful shove. But while we were rolling around the bed laughing, I shivered at the thought of what a trip to Ludowici could mean to my future.

· • · · • · · • ·

When the alarm went off the next morning at 6 o'clock, I was dreaming about Dad. No, not a dream. Make that a nightmare. I was crawling after him, crying hysterically. The look on his face as he walked away left me heartbroken. I woke up teary-eyed. What was his problem? My dad had always been so open-minded.

Why couldn't he accept that his beloved daughter was trapped in a 14-year-old body? Probably because he hadn't read about it in a medical journal.

Sighing, I forced myself to get up, but I couldn't stop thinking about him. We had been father and daughter for eighteen years and had shared a lot of history. Maybe I should try to talk to him one more time. Maybe at graduation. After all, he would be there to get my diploma.

Then there was this thing with Justin. I had always seen him as such an annoying and obnoxious loser around me. But this new protective, concerned Justin I had come to know left me with unsettled feelings. I shook my head and tried to focus my thoughts. Is it possible that Justin might be able to help me convince Dad that his beloved Lindsey was still alive?

I padded barefoot into the bathroom and splashed cold water in my face. Wiping my eyes, I stared at Annabeth's face in the bathroom mirror. "You are oh-so-not Lindsey Anderson." I tore off a few squares of toilet paper and blew my nose. Turning back to the image in the mirror, I shook my finger. "Look at yourself. Yuck! Stringy blonde hair. Big, blah hazel eyes. High cheekbones. Tom-boy flat chest. Runway-model skinny." I took a closer look at her complexion. So smooth. Truly like a baby's bottom. No sign of acne or imperfection anywhere.

I took a step back from the mirror and considered Annabeth's body. Mmm. Doubtful if she could make it as a New York model. And not likely this body could hack it on the soccer field. How about as a gymnast? "Could you balance yourself on a beam?" I asked the girl in the mirror. "Can you sing or dance? If I'm going to be stuck with you, what have you got for us to work with?" That knot rose in my throat.

"Who are you talking to?" Rachel called out through the bathroom door. "Are you all right?"

I blew my nose and tried to speak without my voice quaking. "I'm okay." I glanced back at Annabeth's face. Actually, I wasn't, but I didn't want to be a constant downer in front of my best friend. I needed a happy face for Rachel.

·　　·　　·　　·　　·

I carefully spread strawberry jelly on my English muffin and sat down next to Rachel, my chocoholic friend, who was pouring herself a glass of chocolate milk. "What, no chocolate muffins today?"

Rachel poured me a glass of milk. "I'm cutting back on chocolate for breakfast."

"I find that hard to believe." After Rachel had experienced a chocolate breakfast during a family vacation to Hershey, Pennsylvania, she always had some form of chocolate for breakfast. Her favorite was chocolate chip pancakes with Hershey chocolate syrup.

"My dermatologist said cutting back on the chocolate might improve my acne problem," Rachel said. "So now I only have one thing with chocolate for breakfast."

I rolled my eyes upward, as she swallowed the last drop of chocolate milk. I had to bite my lip so I wouldn't laugh out loud. Rachel's acne problem was a little zit on her chin every month or so. I sipped my milk. "Think we can get on the road soon?"

Rachel clunked her glass on the table. "I don't know what I was thinking when I agreed to do this."

"You were thinking of my happiness."

"I'm sure that's exactly what it was." She stretched her neck in my direction. "Nice-looking tan pants and plaid shirt. Obviously came from a high-end store."

"Yeah, you are so right. Nordstrom, I think. Or maybe Macy's." I took my empty glass over to the sink. Then I pulled out the waistband of the trousers. "They are a little bit loose on me." I looked down at the shoes on my feet and pointed. "So are these Nikes, but I tied them tight, so they won't fall off."

Rachel dropped her cup and plate in the sink. "Isn't it great to have a friend who knows where all the best buys are?"

I stood up. "It's great that I have a best friend who sticks by me no matter what body I'm in." Rachel threw her arms around me and gave me a huge hug. My eyes watered. It was an awesome Bomber-bonding moment.

⸱　　⸱　　⸱　　⸱

Forty-five minutes later, we were in my Mustang convertible, heading south. Even though Annabeth didn't have a driver's license, Rachel let me have the wheel. That's what being best friends is all about—getting your way when it's important. She also combed my hair into a sophisticated style and made sure I had on enough makeup to pass for 16 or older. Sunglasses helped, too. And I made sure I did not exceed the speed limit.

We exited the Interstate at Forsyth and stopped at Hardee's. I could smell the cinnamon and raisin biscuits when we walked through the door. I ordered one and stuck my finger in the warm sugary topping that oozed down the sides. Then I sucked the frosting off my finger and took a big bite of the biscuit. I was beginning to feel a whole lot better.

"Want me to drive now?" Rachel held out her hand for the keys.

I opened the driver's door. "I'm fine, thank you."

"Don't forget, you don't have a driver's license," She pointed out, crawling into the passenger's seat.

I slid in behind the wheel and started the engine. "I've been legally driving for three years."

"What if we get pulled over?" asked Rachel.

"You're my best friend—don't mess it up. Besides, I'm not going to exceed the speed limit or pass in the emergency lane or run any stop signs." I felt like my grandfather must have felt when Dad told him he was too old to drive any more. Give up your car, lose your independence. Besides, my Mustang was my baby.

Rachel began tinkering with the radio. She'd never been able to win an argument with me, even when I was wrong, because she knew I was always right.

•   •   •   •   •

Once we reached Macon, we exited I-75 and headed east on I-16. The rolling hills of the Piedmont soon gave way to the flatness of the coastal plains. The red clay soil turned sandy and white. Oak trees were outnumbered by loblolly pines. We passed lumber trucks on their way to pulp mills and metal shipping crates headed to ports in Savannah or Brunswick.

When we exited I-16 onto state highway 57, Rachel pulled up Google maps on her cell phone.

"I can get us to Reidsville and Glennville," I said. "Then what?"

Rachel touched the map with her finger. "In Glennville, we pick up U.S. Highway 25/301." She paused. "Wow! Do you realize that Ludowici is the only town in Long County?"

I shook my head. "I knew it was the county seat." And a small South Georgia town with a population of less than 3,000.

Rachel glanced up from the map. "Must not be too many people living down there."

I nodded and watched miles of nothing go by until we crossed the Long County line. When folks talked about living in "the sticks," this had to be it. After a few miles, I slowed down and pointed out a road on the right. "That road leads to the Altamaha River."

"How do you know that?" Rachel asked, taking her eyes away from her cell phone screen.

"From Annabeth's diary. She and her friends used to picnic there and go skinny-dipping."

"She wrote that in her diary?" Rachel asked.

I nodded. "Among other things."

"I wouldn't have written anything like that in my diary. No privacy at my house. Sooner or later my brother would stumble across my diary, read it, and broadcast it all over Facebook."

"I guess I've just proven your case, right?" I replied.

"Oh,yeah! What else did you find out?"

"She loved her father. Her life with him sounded idyllic. They were very close. He took her fishing for rooster reds in the Altamaha River, and they went hunting in Raccoon Flat. Some kind of swamp, I think. She was heartbroken when he was killed." Just like me when Mom died. Thank goodness Dad didn't remarry. He never even seriously dated anyone. It was just me and him.

Rachel turned off the radio. "Yeah, I bet, especially after her stepfather turned out to be a pervert."

The outskirts of Ludowici were dotted with abandoned buildings, mobile homes, small churches, and pine forests. At the one traffic light, where there were two gas stations, a Family Dollar Store, and Ludowici Drugs, I turned right onto the town's main street. We passed the Heritage Bank, a Subway, the Southern Hardware Feed and Seed, the Royal Inn, and Lena Mae's Country Cafe. I read on Wikipedia that the main street ran parallel with CSX railroad tracks and led to the big ITT Ranier plant just across the line in Wayne County. The plant was the largest employer in the area.

"This is one small town," remarked Rachel.

"Don't forget it's the county seat." When a Dairy Queen came into view, we decided to take a break. I parked the car, and we went inside. I ordered a medium Peanut Buttercup Blizzard; Rachel settled on a large hot fudge sundae.

A young woman in a red DQ shirt took our orders and kept staring at me. "You from around here?" she asked with a thick South Georgia drawl.

I shook my head. "First time here."

"Funny, I coulda swore I know'd you."

A second young woman, who oozed hot fudge all over the ice cream curl, turned to face me. "Ellie, you know who she looks like? That Shepard girl who left home in the middle of the night, and nobody heard from her, ever again?"

Ellie popped her gum and studied my face. "Yeah, you're right, Leekie, that's exactly who she looks like." She plopped my Blizzard on the counter, along with a long, red plastic spoon. "Well, you know what they say 'bout everyone havin' a twin."

I dug my spoon into the mixture of ice cream and pieces of Reese's Peanut Buttercups, and tried to appear totally absorbed in getting a heaping spoonful into my mouth. Had I been found out? I swallowed and felt the cold slide down my throat and into my stomach. "Does this Shepard family still live around here?" I asked as casually as possible.

Leekie handed the hot fudge sundae to Rachel and wiped her hands on her red apron. "They sure do. At least the mama." She turned around to Ellie, who was wiping off the counter underneath the milkshake machine. "Ain't that right?"

"Yep, I reckon so. She lives all by herself. In that old house on Old Farm Road, you know—southeast of town." Ellie dropped the dishcloth in the sink and cocked her head. "Why you interested?"

"Oh, you just got my curiosity up, when you said I looked like the daughter. I wouldn't want to cross a relative's path and startle them or anything." And we certainly didn't want to waste any time, if Annabeth's mom had moved away or died.

Ellie nodded and raked two banana peels into the trash. "Not to worry 'bout that. She's the only one left down there and don't leave the house for nothing. She's got that hardening of the arteries stuff in her eyes. You know what I mean? She don't see so well."

"There used to be a stepfather." Leekie leaned forward on the counter conspiratorially and lowered her voice. "But he tried a little hanky panky on the deputy sheriff's daughter after a football game one night. Remember that, Ellie? It was the night our boys whupped the team from Jesup. Anyways, that got his butt in jail."

"Yep, and we heard that he accidentally—" She winked at us. "—got beat up a little bit in jail. The sheriff said he must've tripped and fell, but we know better, don't we? Nobody cares much for men like that. Not even prisoners. Sooner or later, somebody will whack him and do him in."

The door to the Dairy Queen opened, and a full-bearded man in faded bib-overalls stomped in and headed to the other end of the counter. Ellie and Leekie moved in his direction. As we pushed open the glass door to leave, the man wiped off his face with a red bandana and ordered five barbecue sandwiches, french-fried onion rings, and one large iced tea.

"Wow!" marveled Rachel, opening the Mustang's passenger door. "Sounds like Annabeth's stepfather got what he deserved."

I cranked the engine and backed out of the parking place. Too bad he couldn't have gotten it a few years earlier—like before he met Annabeth's mom.

"Where to now?" Rachel asked. "Ludowici High?"

"No, I want to see the farm where Annabeth was raised." I felt compelled to do this, but I wasn't sure why.

"Is this absolutely necessary?" Rachel asked.

"I can't go back to Atlanta unless I see it for myself." What was I hoping to find? A life I could fit into? A mother who would love me? I seriously doubted it.

Rachel sighed loudly.

I focused on the small buildings that made up downtown Ludowici. What would it have been like growing up in this rural area of South Georgia? Did everyone know everybody? If they saw your bedroom light on in the middle of the night, did they call the next day to see if you were sick? I drove back to the traffic light and turned right. We passed the Faith Baptist Church and thumped over the railroad tracks, passing the police department, the county tag office, a number of county government offices, past several schools, and the Strangers Cemetery, before edging out of town.

Five miles south of the edge of town, Rachel yelled "That's it!" and pointed at a dirt and gravel road off to the left. "Old Farm Road."

I slammed on the brakes. Tires squealed on the asphalt, as I sharply turned the Mustang onto the road—something I hadn't done since high school. The convertible skidded and slid on the gravel, but managed to remain out of the ditch. I smiled sheepishly at Rachel, who was digging her heels into the floor board.

About three miles down the road, I eased off the gas and slowed as an old, dented mailbox came into view. Squinting in the bright, hot sun, I tried to read the name on the box. "I can't make it out, can you?"

Rachel lowered the window and leaned out to get a closer look at the worn, faded, hand-painted lettering on the side of the box. "Looks like an 'S' and something and then an 'E' and maybe a 'P' but the rest is gone. What do you think?"

"That could be what's left of Shepard. Let's give it a try." I turned right onto a two-rut drive. The weeds and bushes on either side brushed the sides of the car. Rachel raised the window to avoid getting slapped in the face by leaves and branches. Tall, grassy weeds running down the middle of the drive "ka-thunked" against the bumper, as we ran over them. The rough terrain prevented me from driving faster than a crawl, which was slow enough for hordes of gnats to descend on us from the undergrowth. It was obvious that not too many cars went down this drive.

Finally, we pulled into a clearing with half a dozen pecan trees and a medium-sized, wood-frame farm house with several dilapidated outbuildings out back. I had expected to see a rusting old trailer. Over the years, the paint had peeled and flaked off the house, leaving the wood bleached gray from the sun. Several planks on the front porch had rotted through, leaving gaping holes. One of the corner posts holding up the porch roof had given away, and the roof sagged nearly to the ground. The screen door stood haphazardly and seemed ready to fall over at any moment. As I brought the Mustang to a halt and turned off the engine, it felt like someone was squeezing my heart tightly with both hands.

"What are you doing?" squeaked Rachel. "You've seen it, let's go!"

I opened my door and started to slide out, but Rachel grabbed my arm. "Rachel, let go!"

"Lindsey, are you out of your mind? Get back in here and shut the door."

"Let go!" Rachel released her grip. "I'm going up to that front door and see if anyone is home. You can either stay or come with me." It was impossible for me to make her understand what was drawing me toward that house. I didn't understand myself why I was compelled to get closer to Annabeth's past.

Waiting outside the car, I stared at the spooky, foreboding house. I swatted a deer fly that tried to bite my arm and blew at a cloud of buzzing gnats invading my face. Did I look like lunch to these insects or what? I looked questioningly at Rachel.

Rachel opened her door and slid out. "Okay, I'll go. It's a best friend's duty to look after her friend, even a loony one. Besides, I'm not staying in this car by myself."

I didn't respond. Like a robot zombie, I walked towards the porch. I couldn't help myself.

Rachel shut the car door and followed me. "I just have one question, Lindsey."

"What?"

"If Annabeth's mother does live here, what then?"

"I don't know. Let's just see what happens." And although I wouldn't admit it to Rachel, I was so scared, my knees trembled, and my heart seemed to have fallen to the bottom of my stomach. But I kept walking, and my best friend followed four steps behind.

Dodging gaping holes in the porch floor, like land mines in a field, I reached the screen door and knocked softly. Snarls and growls sounded from within the house. I jumped back just as the screen door burst open with a furor. A fast-moving black mass of terror rose from the ground, striking me in the chest and knocking me down. Was my throat about to be ripped open? This body was going to bleed to death on the steps of Annabeth's home. How fitting.

A screaming Rachel grabbed a fallen rail post to hit the vicious mongrel that was jumping all over me. But before she could strike the barking, snapping animal, it let out a startled yelp, jumped down and began whining and wiggling his backside. Rachel dropped the stick and stood there dumbfounded.

"I'm so scared I nearly peed my pants," Rachel said, cowering against a porch post.

Shaking and crying from fright and relief, I managed to get to my feet and fend off the huge, ugly hound dog that was trying to lick my face.

"If that ain't the damnedest thing I ever seen!" A middle-aged woman stood in the yard pointing a double-barreled shotgun in our direction. "Bruiser don't like no trespassers. He never lets one get away unless I call him off."

A chill went up my spine. If Bruiser had been around when Annabeth lived here, then he would remember how her body smelled.

"Bruiser, heel boy." The woman cocked the gun and took a step closer to the porch.

Bruiser sat at my feet, thumped his tail on the worn, wooden porch boards and whined. I nudged him gently with my toe. "Run along, Bruiser," I hissed at him.

Bruiser reluctantly crept down the decrepit porch steps and sat next to the old woman. Her dull gray hair was pulled back in a bun, exposing a weathered, wrinkled face. She wore loose-fitting, well-worn jeans and a pale, faded denim shirt with the sleeves rolled up to the elbows. "I don't know why Bruiser took a liken to you girlie, but you're mighty lucky. The last fellow on that porch near got his arm chewed off." She jabbed the barrel of her gun in the air. "Now git back in that fancy car and git off my property."

Rachel grabbed my elbow and tried to lead me down the steps, but I shook away her hand. "We're sorry if we surprised you, ma'am. We're friends of your daughter, Annabeth."

The woman lowered her shotgun half a foot and glared at us. "Ain't got no daughter."

"Annabeth Shepard isn't your daughter?"

"My daughter's dead."

Rachel and I crossed the rickety porch and went down the steps, carefully avoiding the holes. But instead of going to the car, I walked toward the old woman. "What are you doing?" Rachel hissed. "Let's get out of here."

"Okay, you get in the car. Here!" I tossed her the keys. "You said you wanted to drive."

"I'm not going without you."

"Give me five minutes."

Rachel scowled at me, backed up to the car, opened the driver's door and slid in behind the wheel.

As I approached the woman, Bruiser started running circles around me and yelping happily.

"Bruiser, git over here." The woman snapped her fingers and pointed to the ground by her side. The dog crawled over to her and sat, watching me and wagging his tail.

"Mrs. Shepard—"

"My name is Mrs. Crowe."

"That's right, Mr. Shepard died and you remarried." Even though I knew she would be within her rights to shoot me for trespassing, I took a step closer. I couldn't help myself.

"Stop right there, girlie. That's close enough. What do you want?"

"Annabeth's forgiven you for not believing her." I held my breath and waited for the shotgun blast that would knock me down.

The woman threw the back of her hand to her mouth and gasped.

She came right up to me and grabbed my wrist so tightly I yelped. Bruiser stood up and whined.

"Who are you, girlie? Coming out here to my home and saying you're friends with my daughter?" Her face edged so close to mine, I could smell peanut butter on her breath. She frowned and squinted her eyes.

"I'm—uh—just a friend," I stammered, my heart pounding in my chest. Was this woman insane?

Annabeth's mother released my wrist and reached for my face. Her callused hand felt rough against my cheek. She grabbed a fistful of my hair and wrapped it around her fingers. "I don't see well at all any more, but you shore do remind me of my Annabeth."

I held my breath and swallowed hard. Out of the corner of my eye, I could see Rachel standing hesitantly by the car.

The woman poked my shoulder with a bony finger. "But you don't sound like my Annabeth. You ain't from South Georgia. No accent."

I watched her warily. Even though the shotgun was now pointed at the ground, I didn't want to do or say anything to excite her. "Several folks in Atlanta think we look alike."

Mrs. Crowe dropped her hand and stepped back. "Is it true then? You know my girl Annabeth for real? And she don't hate me?"

I relaxed and shook my head. "No, Ma'am, she only hates Mr. Crowe for doing her wrong."

Mrs. Crow's face scrunched up, as though she were in great pain. In just a matter of seconds, I watched her go from a woman who could blow heads off, to a fragile, frightened person. "She understands you were too afraid to tell him to leave."

A muted anguished cry escaped from Mrs. Crow's throat, as she turned her back to me. Then her shoulders began to shake as she broke into soft, gulping sobs. Not sure what was the right thing to do, I hesitantly approached her and slowly placed my hands on her shoulders. Just as quickly as her emotions had opened up, they stopped. She wiped her eyes and nose on her sleeve, and turned around.

"I was glad she left before he hurt her anymore." Mrs. Crowe stared at me from red eyes brimming with tears. "It didn't matter what he did to me as long as she was safe. Did she understand that?"

"Yes, I think she did," I said. "Maybe not at first, but later she did."

"I should have called the sheriff on him, but I just couldn't do it." Her eyes pleaded for me to understand.

After an awkward period of silence, she nodded and her face changed, again. Frown lines softened and signs of sorrow and distress disappeared into a smile. It was downright eerie. The woman must have multiple personalities or something.

"That was real nice of you to drive all the way down here from Atlanta," Mrs. Crowe said. "I guess Annabeth was afraid to come with ya'll and I can't say I blame her." She motioned to Rachel. "Why don't you and your friend come inside and sit a spell with me, and tell me more about my daughter." She turned and headed around the corner of the house.

I looked at Rachel. She looked anxious, and I knew she wanted to get out of here. Part of me was with her, but the other part wanted to stay and see what I could find out about Annabeth's life. I shrugged and followed Annabeth's mother around the house to a back porch. I heard Rachel's steps behind me.

"If she shoots us and dismembers our bodies, you'll be sorry," Rachel said, coming up beside me.

"A single woman living alone in the middle of nowhere has to be careful," I said.

Rachel grunted and mumbled something under her breath, but I didn't understand what she said, which was probably a good thing.

Unlike the front of the house, the back porch looked cared for. Baskets of geraniums and impatiens in full bloom hung from the porch rafters. Four rockers lined the shady porch. Maybe the unsightly appearance of the front of the house was to dissuade visitors from dropping by.

Mrs. Crowe waited for us to follow her up the back steps and through the back door into a kitchen that was faded and worn, but clean. A floor fan stood in the doorway to circulate the warm, humid air. "I don't get much company nowadays," she said, washing her hands at the sink. "A few ladies from my church circle drop by from time to time." She dried off her hands with a faded hand towel. "And I don't do much cooking, since there's only one of me now. But if there's one thing I dearly love when the days start getting warmer is homemade lemonade, and I just made me some this morning."

We took our glasses of lemonade out onto the porch and sat down in the rockers. Sitting outside in this humidity was like trying to breathe liquid, but it was cooler on the porch than inside the house. Even sweating didn't make you cooler because there was no evaporation. I sipped my lemonade and rocked, and tried to picture Annabeth out here in this heat. Then I laughed at the irony because Annabeth was out here in this heat.

Mrs. Crowe joined us on the porch with a plate of banana bread. "Billie Ruth brought it by two days ago. Bless her heart. She has air-conditioning and doesn't mind heating up her oven when the day is warm. There's some good people in this town."

Rachel waited for me to taste the banana bread first. I took a small bite, expecting it to be dried out and yucky, but it was still moist and delicious. I took a second, bigger bite. "Mmm, this is good."

"Yep, Billie Ruth's banana bread recipe is known as the best around these parts." Mrs. Crowe leaned back in her rocker and sipped her lemonade. "Now talk to me about Annabeth. What's she doing?"

"Uh—she's working in the hospitality industry." Geez, but I barely got that out of my mouth.

"Doing what?"

"Uh—" I looked at Rachel helplessly.

"Customer relations," Rachel said. "And entertainment," she added.

Mrs. Crowe smiled and bit her lower lip. A tear rolled down her cheek. She wiped it off with the back of her hand. "I'm mighty glad. I was afraid she would get mixed up with some bad people."

"I can promise you that she isn't involved with any bad people," I said. At least not currently and has no plans to get back into it.

"Does Annabeth ever talk about her home in Ludowici?" her mother asked.

I exchanged glances with Rachel. "She really loved her father."

Mrs. Crowe rocked back and forth. The porch floorboards squeaked as she rocked. "Yeah, Hiram was a good man. A very good man." She rocked a little bit more. "He doted on his daughter. Shame he had to die so young."

Her face literally deflated in front of me. The only sounds were from the rocker moving on the squeaky boards.

Later, as we walked back to the Mustang, Mrs. Crowe thanked us for stopping by and apologized for our less-than-warm reception. "There's some crazy and mean people out there in this world."

I nodded. Yeah, like Tony and Dante.

"I'm here by myself with just Bruiser for company. If something happened to me, no one would notice or even care." She paused and swallowed. "You tell Annabeth that I love her," Mrs. Crow said. "I know she won't ever be able to forgive me for what I did, but maybe one day she'll come back to Ludowici."

"I'll certainly tell her that." But I knew that Annabeth would never return to this town. Trying to live Annabeth's life in Ludowici was not what I wanted. I knew that now. Before I got in the car, I pulled Annabeth's backpack from the backseat and reached in, pulling out a thick envelope. "I almost forgot, Annabeth asked me to give this to you." I handed the envelope to Annabeth's mother.

Rachel frowned and looked puzzled.

I slid into the passenger's seat and slammed the door.

While Mrs. Crow ripped open the envelope, Rachel turned the car around in the yard and headed down the jungle driveway.

In the side mirror, I watched Mrs. Crow pull out the contents of the envelope and look up with a shocked expression. I reached over and blew the horn and waved as we drove out of sight.

"Lindsey Anderson, what was in that envelope?" Rachel asked.

"Money. Thousands of dollars that I found hidden in an inside zippered pocket of the backpack."

"What?" Rachel raised a questioning eyebrow. "You took money from Tony's bag?"

"Not me, but Annabeth must have. She and her friend Neeley Hill planned to leave town with all of the money to start a new life. She wrote about returning to Ludowici to see her mother. I'd like to think she would want to give some of the money to her mom."

"So, you're thinking she hid the money, but was killed before she could go back for it?" Rachel said.

"That's exactly right."

We didn't say much during the long ride back to Atlanta. Which was fine with me, since I had a lot to think about.

CHAPTER TWENTY-THREE
GRADUATION DAY

My throat ached, and my eyes filled with tears at the sight of my friends and classmates dressed in their royal blue caps and gowns. As I watched them huddled outside the auditorium, posing for photos and hugging friends, I wanted to scream and howl in despair. Rip and shred the way-too-big Neiman Marcus sundress Rachel had loaned me for her graduation day. But I lowered my head and walked right by them. Not a single person gave me a second glance. On this day that I had looked forward to for the last four years, I was a stranger. A nameless nobody.

Twenty feet from the auditorium entrance, I saw my dad talking to Rachel's parents. My heartbeat increased, and it was difficult to breathe. Dad turned in my direction. When our eyes locked, I reached out my hand to him. But he did a 180-degree turn and disappeared into a blue sea of caps and gowns. Blinking back tears, I hurried into the auditorium and claimed an aisle seat near the back.

It was okay, I told myself, and opened the graduation program. Trying to tune out the happy chatter of everyone around me, I focused on the page in front of me. But I couldn't read through my tears. Instead, I thumbed aimlessly through the program pages, waiting for my vision to clear.

I thought back to last week's visit with Neeley in the hospital. Rachel had dropped me off at St. Mary's after Justin told me she was getting released. When I pushed open the door to her room, Neeley was watching television. As soon as she saw me, she literally leaped out of bed to give me a hug.

"Annabeth! I knew you'd come!" She hugged me, again. "I saw on the news about the shoot-out at the MARTA station. Girlfriend, are you okay?"

"I'm doing great." I touched her chin. "Looks like you're going to be all right." The left side of her face was still a little bit bruised, and her left eye was slightly swollen, but she looked better than I thought she would.

She pulled me over to her bed. "Sit. Tell me all."

Sitting side by side, like old friends, I told her about being chased and shot at by Tony and Dante. She shrieked and giggled and clapped her hands, when she heard about the train slamming into the money bag. "I wish I'd been there to see that."

I reached out and grabbed her hand. "Trust me, you were a whole lot safer here." She squeezed my hand and grinned.

"I hear you're being released tomorrow?"

Neeley released my hand and nodded. "Uh-huh. I had a choice of going into foster care or calling my family."

"You called your family?" I knew from Annabeth's journal that Neeley's mother had died when she was twelve. Her grandparents took her home to live with them, but Neeley eventually ran away because they seemed too strict.

She sighed. "Yeah, I did. My aunt is coming tomorrow from Macon and taking me back to live with my grandparents. It won't be easy, but fricking better than being a sex slave for Tony. I plan to work hard in school, make good grades, and graduate."

I nodded. That was my plan, too. I would just have to suck it up, repeat four years of high school somewhere, and hopefully go to college. Majoring in social work or criminal justice was a possibility. Maybe go to law school. But more than anything, I wanted to make a difference. I wanted to fight against sex trafficking and help victims find better lives.

Neeley gave me her grandparents' address and a good-bye hug. "As soon as I know where I'll be living, I'll send you my address," I explained. "Hopefully, I can be placed with a kind, caring family."

•　　•　　•　　•　　•

When I finally looked up from the graduation program, I caught a glimpse of Dad walking down the aisle between Al McCracken and Steve Hopkins. This time, when Dad's eyes met mine, he paused in mid-stride. He didn't smile, but he didn't look at me like I was an alien from Mars. Or like he didn't know if he should scream and run in terror or report me to Homeland Security.

Not taking his eyes off of me, Dad grabbed Dr. McCracken's arm and whispered in his ear. Dr. McCracken nodded in my direction and steered Dad down the aisle toward seats closer to the front. I turned back to my program, wiping tears off the pages. After a few minutes, I was able to read the names of my graduating friends, where they were going to college, and what scholarships they had been awarded.

Next time I looked up, I caught Dad staring at me over his shoulder. Trembling all over, I jumped up and ran outside. Leaning against an oak tree, I began to feel sorry for myself. All of my friends were graduating today. It should be a happy day for me. Yay me! Here I stood with my life in turmoil. My friends would spend the summer packing for college, and, in a few days, I would leave Rachel's and head to a foster care home. Most likely, we would never see each other again. A tear rolled down my cheek. What a wuss I had become.

Then suddenly Justin was by my side, his arm around my shoulders. "What's wrong?"

I leaned into him. "My dad. It hurts the way he looks at me, you know? Like I'm a stranger."

Justin gave me a hug. "I know, Lindsey, but if it were the other way around, and a young man came up and told you he was your dead father—well, you would have your own doubts and concerns, wouldn't you?"

I pulled back from him and concentrated on my feet and Rachel's black sandals, which were a size too big for me. "Maybe." But if Dad told me intimate details of our life together as father and daughter, wouldn't I give him the benefit of the doubt? I really wasn't sure. This whole thing was so bizarre and unbelievable, and it was happening to me.

Justin reached for my hand. I moved my eyes from my feet, up the length of his gown to his face and the tassel that swung from his cap. His hand felt warm and damp. And comforting. As much as I had loathed Justin throughout high school, I was now starting to like him. Really like him. I would miss him, too.

"I know I'm a little annoying, even somewhat obnoxious, but I've liked you since middle school, when they promoted me up two grades." he whispered in my ear. "I can't stand the thought of not seeing you, again."

My cheeks began to heat up. Was it possible that I felt the same way about him, too? Was he actually liking the new me? This whole thing was complicated. Before, he liked Lindsey and Lindsey's body. Now I was still Lindsey, but Lindsey in Annabeth's body. I was a Cherry Coke in a Yahoo bottle. Just where was he going with this? "Justin, I'm sorry you felt it was necessary to be an asshole to get my attention."

"Ah, but, as you pointed out—it was only negative attention."

I smiled. How funny. Over the last few weeks, I had discovered a new Justin that I didn't know. A new Justin that I liked. Was that true for Justin? Was he liking the new Lindsey?

He lowered his head, his mouth next to my ear. "Do you think you could go for a guy who has aspirations to be another Bill Gates?"

"Maybe." Suddenly I felt like a tongue-tied, shy 14-year-old girl.

"If you think that might be possible, not only will I forgive you for running off and leaving me to be beaten up by your pimp, but I'd be willing to wait for you to graduate from high school."

My cheeks burned. I pulled my hand out of his. "Justin!"

"What? Now that you have this new 14-year-old body, we can't be friends?" He pretended to be offended.

"I—uh—I—uh—" The words wouldn't come out. I could not think of anything sharp or witty to say. What was happening to me? In Lindsey's body, I always had a smart comeback. I always knew what to say.

The orchestral sounds of "Pomp and Circumstance" drifted from the open auditorium doors, and the line of graduates began marching through the entrance. "That's my cue," Justin said. "We'll have to continue this conversation later."

I shook my head and headed back to the auditorium, but stopped when I saw local TV and newspaper reporters standing next to a white passenger van. The van door slid open, and five men and women with camcorders and briefcases exited the vehicle. While one man unfolded a wheelchair on the sidewalk, two others helped another man out of the van and into the wheelchair. When they moved back, I gasped. It was Dr. Epting, still recovering from his beating. The ghostbusters had arrived. And I knew they weren't here to cover graduation.

I inched my way over to another oak tree near the van and eavesdropped unashamedly on their conversation.

"Let me see if I have this right, Dr. Epting," a female reporter from the Atlanta daily newspaper said. "You think the soul of a deceased East Lake High senior is occupying the body of a 14-year-old sex trafficking victim?"

"We're not 100 percent certain. But once we get her to our laboratories and run tests, we'll know more," Dr. Epting said. He had on his usual pastel attire—a pale gray sports coat, lavender shirt, and pink and gray-striped tie.

Leaning against the tree for support, I suddenly became aware that I had been holding my breath, which burst from my lungs with an audible gasp. I thought that once I left the hospital, the ghostbusters would remain in California. *Holy crap! I'm a juicier story than I knew.*

"I wouldn't mind waking up in a younger body," said a 40-something female TV reporter.

"If I take her photo, will she show up in the picture?" asked a newspaper photographer.

"Don't be ridiculous. She's not a vampire!" said a woman standing behind Dr. Epting.

That woman was obviously one of the ghostbusters. I took a quick peek at her.

"When will we get a chance to talk to her?" the newspaper reporter asked.

"Just stick with us,' said Dr. Epting, as one of the parapsychologists pushed him toward the auditorium. "She's here at graduation."

What was I going to do? Sneak away? No, this was my graduation, and I wasn't going to miss it. I slipped into the auditorium along with my former classmates. Only a few of them gave me a glance. Feeling like a cat burglar, I went up the stairs to the auditorium balcony and found a seat in the rear. From here I could observe Dr. Epting and the ghostbusters, who were standing in the back of the auditorium—no doubt searching for me.

As my high school class marched down the aisle, I was overcome with emotion. My friends would be getting their diplomas, and I was hiding in the balcony.

After the last graduate sat down, the men and women's chorus sang the alma mater, the commencement speeches were made, academic awards were presented, and degrees were conferred. The principal stepped up to the podium and waited. The auditorium went silent.

"Just a few weeks ago, one of our top graduating seniors and star soccer player collapsed on the playing field after kicking the winning goal for the state championship. Lindsey Anderson died at St. Mary's that same evening. This morning we would like to present her diploma with highest honors posthumously to her father, Dr. Reginald Anderson."

As Dad walked to the podium to receive my diploma, a thunderous applause broke out throughout the auditorium, and everyone jumped to their feet. I had promised myself I would control my emotions, but it was like being caught up in a riptide. I was overwhelmed. I cried for my dad, and I cried for me and the life I had lost. A grandmotherly woman in the seat next to mine—who was crying, too—offered me a tissue, which I gratefully accepted, and quietly blew my nose.

Clutching my diploma in one hand and wiping his eyes with the other, Dad made his way back to his seat, where Dr. McCracken gave him a hug and clapped him on the back. Dad looked around the auditorium before he sat down. Was he looking for me?

After the ceremony was over, exuberant new graduates tossed their hats jubilantly into the air and burst through the auditorium doors to the outside world. I quickly left the balcony, in hopes of getting away before anyone spotted me. But when I reached the bottom of the balcony steps and fled out the side door, Dr. Epting, his team of parapsychologists, and a number of reporters and photographers were waiting on the sidewalk.

Dr. Epting lifted his bandaged arm and pointed straight at me. "There she is!"

Reporters and photographers stampeded over to me with cameras clicking and flashes exploding. Before I could escape, reporters shoved microphones into my face and yelled out their questions.

"Are you Lindsey Anderson reincarnated in the body of Annabeth Shepherd?"

"Did Annabeth and Lindsey know each other before they died?"

"Where is the real Miss Shepherd?"

I shook my head, covered up my ears and gaped at the expectant, determined faces of the media, and at the shocked puzzled faces of new graduates, their families, and friends pouring out of the auditorium. Over the heads of the media, I saw Rachel waving her arms, trying to reach me through the crowd. Dad stood next to her, frowning and looking worried. I also saw the smirky, satisfied face of Dr. Epting. Then I felt the reassuring grip of Justin's hand on my arm. Somehow, he had made his way through the hordes.

Goose bumps broke out on my arms. My stomach tightened. I sighed and cleared my throat. Guess this was it. The day of reckoning. Time to decide which road in life I would go down. Dropping my hands from my ears, I licked my lips and opened my mouth. An eerie silence spread through the gathering crowd.

"My name is Annabeth Shepherd." I paused, considering my next words carefully.

A reporter from one of the local radio stations waved his microphone under my nose. "So, there's two of you in that body?"

I pushed away his microphone. "I'm a teenage runaway from a small town."

A petite blonde lifted her mini-recorder in my direction. "Why did you run away?"

"My stepfather molested me." I heard a few gasps in the crowd. "After arriving in Atlanta, I met some bad people. I made some bad choices. I regret to say that I became a sex trafficking victim and a drug addict."

Murmurs went up throughout the group of reporters. "I am one of 1.6 million children who run away from home each year. Any young girl is at risk of being enslaved for sex. The average time it takes a sex trafficker to approach a runaway is only 48 hours."

"Why didn't you just go back home?" the blonde asked.

I sighed. "That wasn't an option. Your pimp owns you. You can't get away. I tried to escape by stealing my pimp's drug money."

A twenty-something male with shoulder-length hair—probably from the student newspaper—yelled out, "Well, no wonder he tried to kill you. What were you thinking?"

Justin squeezed my shoulder. I clinched my jaw and smiled. "I was thinking I could use the money to get out of Atlanta and save myself."

"You're lucky to be alive," said a middle-age woman in a green dress.

"Yes, I owe my life to the doctors and nurses in St. Mary's ER." Justin squeezed my hand. I squeezed back.

"Is it true that you came here because you were supposed to graduate today?" the long-haired student asked. "Miss Anderson?"

I glared at him. "I told you, I am Miss Shepherd. Dr. Steve Hopkins, one of the doctors who saved my life, invited me to see his son graduate." I held up Justin's hand and smiled. "This is Justin Hopkins."

A gray-bearded man stepped forward, pointing his microphone at Justin. "You knew Lindsey Anderson?"

Justin blinked. "Well, yes . . ."

More murmurs went up.

"Isn't it true that Miss Shepherd claimed to be Miss Anderson?" asked the blonde.

My hands trembled. I could not believe it. Were they not going to let this go?

Justin opened his mouth to respond, but his father stepped out of nowhere between me and Justin, and whispered, "Allow me."

The media pressed forward like buzzards going after a road kill.

"I am Dr. Steve Hopkins."

"Is it true or not, Doc?" asked the gray-bearded man.

Dr. Hopkins cleared his throat. "Like many patients regaining consciousness after a life-threatening injury, Miss Shepherd was delirious, confused, and not fully aware of anything she was saying. Just last week, I had a patient wake up from surgery and tell me his wife was sleeping with a two-headed alien from another galaxy." The media laughed.

Dad stepped out of the crowd to my right. He crossed his arms across his chest. Our eyes locked for one second, before I turned back to the media.

"I just want to add that although Lindsey Anderson died at St. Mary's, I was saved from a life of sex trafficking. But there are still girls out there—some as young as 10 years old—being sold online and forced to have sex with men for just $10 a trick. My former pimp and many of the other pimps in Atlanta are drug dealers looking to make extra money by selling young girls. They say you can only sell a dime bag once, but you can sell a 10-year-old girl over and over, again."

I thought I heard some gasps coming from the crowd. That was good. Everyone needed to know what was going on in Atlanta. Something needed to be done to stop it. "Fortunately for me, I have been given a second chance at life. I don't plan to screw it up. I was addicted to drugs, but now I'm clean. My new life goals are to graduate from high school and go to college."

The middle-age reporter pushed her way forward. "But noted psychiatrist Bill Epting says you really are Lindsey Anderson—that Miss Anderson's soul has control of Miss Shepherd's body."

I tried to look as shocked as possible. "That's absurd! Dr. Hopkins explained how confused I was. What part did you not understand?"

"Oh, please, Miss Anderson!" yelled Dr. Epting from the rear of the church. "Drop the facade!"

I looked several reporters in the eye, then pointed at Dr. Epting. "Look," I began, "I don't know what he told you, but it's not true. I promise you that I am Annabeth Shepherd. If somebody else was in my body, wouldn't I know it?"

A female reporter holding a microphone and shadowed by a young man with a camera stepped forward. "You weren't involved with the shooting at the MARTA station?"

I pulled myself up tall. "Do you want the truth or not?"

"Yes," called out the reporters and photographers.

"I gave it to you. My life hit bottom here in Atlanta. The doctors and nurses at St. Mary's saved my life. Lt. Richards and the Atlanta police department used my information to take down a drug and sex trafficking ring, and arrest two murderers."

Dad actually smiled at me. Stress began to drain from my body. "I want to thank everyone who gave me my life back. Now, if there are no more questions, then I'm sure everyone would like to get back to celebrating this graduation day. These graduates should be your headline story."

As I turned away from the media and parapsychologists, they slowly started to leave. Shouting for them not to go, Dr. Epting rolled his wheelchair after them. Rachel came out of the crowd and gave me a hug.

"You did great!" said Rachel. "You were so calm and cool! I would have passed out. I love you!"

"I love you, too," I said softly.

"You're coming to the graduation party, aren't you?" Rachel asked.

"Yes, of course. Justin is taking me." I looked at him. "Right?"

Justin grinned and nodded.

"Great!" said Rachel. "We are the East Lake Bombers!"

"We rock!" I responded, following Justin and Rachel toward her car.

"Hey, Dad, thanks for helping me out," Justin called out to Dr. Hopkins.

I sucked in a deep breath, as my own dad stepped up to my side. "Please, could we talk? I want to apologize for my earlier behavior." He looked at Justin and Rachel expectantly.

"Oh, yeah, right—uh—I believe we'll wait for you over there," Justin said, pointing to the edge of the parking lot. "Hey, Dr. McCracken, how about you taking a photo of me with my dad?" They moved away, leaving me and Dad alone.

Dad watched them leave. He looked down at his shoes and rubbed the back of his neck. "I'm not good at this touchy-feely stuff."

"Yeah, I know," I said softly.

He cleared his throat. "I've done a lot of thinking since that day in the apartment. I've decided to form a foundation—the Lindsey Anderson Memorial Foundation. I wasn't sure where the focus should be at first, but now I know."

What!? Dad had named a foundation after me. My eyes stung and a lump rose in my throat. I swallowed hard.

"I want to help teenage girls get off the streets and make something of their lives." His voice cracked.

I chewed my lower lip and fought back the tears.

Dad reached for my hand. "And—" He looked at his feet. "—uh—I would like to become your legal guardian. What do you say?"

It took a few seconds for my brain to comprehend what I was hearing. "Oh, yes!" Impulsively, I grabbed him around the neck and kissed him on the cheek. "Thank you!"

After a few hesitant seconds, he hugged me back. "You're welcome."

"You don't know how much this means to me," I said.

He rubbed his hand tenderly across my cheek and kissed me on the forehead. His eyes welled with tears. "Give me some time," he said hoarsely. "We'll have to take this new relationship in baby steps. Is that all right?" He held my hand to his lips and kissed my fingers. "I'll call my lawyer in the morning and get him going on the paper work. You're still at Rachel's?"

I nodded. "Dr. McCracken worked it out with DFACS."

"I'll call you, Monday, Lin . . . um . . . Annabeth." He turned and walked away.

A few tears rolled down my cheeks, as I watched him leave. He was making no promises, but it was a beginning. I'd grab hold of what he'd thrown to me, and I wouldn't let go.

Justin returned to my side. "Are you crying, again?"

"Graduating from high school is an emotional moment," I said, wiping my eyes and watching dozens of proud family members and friends snap photos of grinning new graduates.

"Yeah, I see that." He said, as we headed toward Rachel's car. "Tell me, Lindsey . . ."

"Annabeth . . ."

He halted in the middle of the sidewalk. "Annabeth? Are you sure this is what you want?"

"Yes. From now on, I am Annabeth Shepard from Ludowici."

"Then Annabeth it will be." We strolled arm in arm. "So, Annabeth, now that you are grateful for a chance to begin a new life, what's the first thing you plan to do?"

I pulled him to a halt. "What do you think? Start high school at East Lake in the fall."

"You're not returning to Ludowici?" He looked very relieved. "Thank goodness."

"At one point, I thought picking up the pieces of Annabeth's life in South Georgia might be a possibility, but after visiting the town and meeting her mother and seeing the house . . ."

Justin squeezed my hand. "You really drove down to Ludowici?"

I nodded. "Rachel went with me."

He threw back his head and laughed. "I'm sorry I missed out on that road trip."

Justin wrapped his arms around me and hugged me tight. I felt safe and loved. I didn't want the warm, fuzzy feeling to end.

Justin stepped back and clasped my hands in his. "I suppose you'll ace your way through high school and graduate at the top of your class? Make a perfect score on the SAT, win a soccer scholarship to Stanford, make the Olympic women's soccer team, graduate with highest honors from college, and have a wonderful life?"

I took a deep breath and chewed my lower lip. "This time around, like you told me once, my life will be different."

"How's that?"

"I've been playing soccer for eight years, Justin. I loved it and I was very good at it." I pulled my hand from his and stopped walking.

"But Annabeth's body has never played soccer. This body might not be able to play soccer as well as Lindsey. And I can accept that."

Justin smiled and squeezed my hand. "I'm glad that you've come to realize that."

I smiled. How sweet. He cared. "Justin, it's okay. Annabeth was a track star in middle school, and she loved to run. Didn't this body do a good job of running from Dante and Tony? And this body was in bad shape at the time. I'm thinking I might even try gymnastics or dancing or playing a musical instrument."

"The possibilities are endless!" we chorused together and laughed.

I looked him straight in the eye. "The next few years are going to be exciting. Sort of like Christmas morning."

"Huh?" Justin raised his eyebrow.

"Each present under the tree has the promise of containing something great. And if I open one that doesn't have what I hoped for, then I'll open another one. Sooner or later, I will discover what this body does well."

"Yes, I get it! Then you'll throw all of your time and energy into making Annabeth's body the best it can be. I know it won't be easy."

"No, it won't." I paused. What was I saying? "This body is totally me now. I can do anything."

"You know, I don't doubt it one bit." He opened the rear door of his family's Ford Echo. "Shall we go party now?"

I slid into the backseat and buckled up. I smiled at Justin's dad. "Thank you for giving me a ride to the party, Dr. Hopkins."

"It is my pleasure, Annabeth." As soon as Justin was seated beside me, Dr. Hopkins started the car.

Bridget Hopkins looked at me from the passenger's seat. "I'm glad you're going to the party with Justin. Do you think you can keep him out of trouble?"

I laughed. "I'll do the best I can, Mrs. Hopkins." Justin squeezed my hand. I looked out my window and whispered, "Annabeth, if you're listening, I promise to take good care of your body. We're going to be the best we can be!"

"Lindsey."

The voice sounded faraway. Like maybe outside the car. "Justin? Was that you?" I asked.

"Was that me what?"

"Did you say something?"

Justin looked at me strangely. "I didn't stay anything. What did you think I said?"

"You didn't call my name?"

Justin shifted in his seat and frowned. "It wasn't me."

"Lindsey."

The voice sounded louder. Someone was calling my name. "There it was, again," I whispered. "Didn't you hear it?"

Justin shook his head. "Nope. Nothing."

"Guess I imagined it." I reached into my purse and pulled out a small notebook.

"What's that?" Justin asked, touching the cover.

"I bought this to use as a journal. I want to write down everything about my new life."

Justin took the book from me and thumbed through the empty pages. "Like a diary?"

I shrugged. "Sort of." I lowered my voice so Justin's parents couldn't hear what I was saying. I wasn't too worried, as they were conversing quite loudly about their summer vacation plans. "I want to write about my life in Annabeth's body. You know, in case one day a new person inhabits this body." Then she can read my journal and see how really good my life was."

"That's a great idea, but I doubt if this body could handle another body swap." He glanced towards his parents, then he leaned over and gently kissed my lips.

It was a nice, soft kiss. A perfectly sweet kiss. Something inside me tingled. Maybe this starting-life-over thing wouldn't be too bad after all.

"I don't think so, either."

What? This time the whispery voice—definitely female— was louder in my head. But no one was in the backseat with me except Justin. I gasped. "Who said that?"

Justin, who had been grinning from ear to ear after the kiss, looked at me in surprise. "Who said what?"

A chill went up my spine. I had a very bad ache in the pit of my stomach. This was not happening. "Oh, no," I whispered. It just couldn't be. I suddenly felt like I was totally freaking losing it.

"Lindsey, it's me, Annabeth!"

AUTHOR'S NOTE

The idea for *Not Myself Today* began germinating in my brain in the 1990s. My protagonist in that first draft was a 58-year-old woman—a well-known, highly-regarded cancer researcher—who was killed in a hit-and-run and woke up in the body of a teenage hooker. But I didn't know anything about teenage prostitution in Atlanta. Time to start researching.

Of special interest to me during several years of research were stories written by investigative reporter Jane O. Hansen and published in the *Atlanta Journal and Constitution* in January 2001—a series called "Selling Atlanta's Children" that documented child prostitution in Atlanta.

Hansen began her series with a courtroom scene in which she described a female defendant escorted into the courtroom with shackles around her ankles. The young girl—dressed in flip-flops and a jail-issued jumpsuit—had been in and out of an Atlanta jail for months. She and her older sister were alleged prostitutes and chronic runaways; no one knew what to do with them. Just 10 years old, the girl quietly told the judge she wanted to go home. Then, as she rubbed her eyes with balled up fists, she began to cry. I was horrified that a sex trafficking victim could be that young.

The average age of children who first become sex trafficking victims in the United States is 11-14 years old. Child sex trafficking is not just a metro Atlanta problem or a Georgia problem. It is a national problem.

Like Hansen, I thought that sex trafficking was dominated by young Asian women brought to the United States and forced to pay back their transportation fees through sexual slavery. But Hansen soon discovered that sex trafficking is a homegrown problem throughout the United States. Many American-born girls are forced to work the streets as prostitutes, controlled by men who house, feed, and clothe them, and then sell them to other men for sex.

After an editor at a writers' conference encouraged me to rewrite *Not Myself Today* as a young adult book, my protagonist became an 18-year-old high school soccer star, who dies on the field after kicking the winning goal. She wakes up in the body of a 14-year-old sex trafficking victim—a teenage runaway, who ended up in Atlanta, where she was tricked into becoming a sex slave.

Which girls are at risk of becoming a child sex trafficking victim? Runaways. Girls having issues and problems at home. Maybe their parents or guardians seem too strict or they are abusive. Or maybe the girls lack love and attention.

Today, social media is a common recruitment tool used by child sex traffickers. Here young girls can connect with men online. Men who convince them that they will love them and take care of them. Once a sex trafficker lures a girl away from home, she can be forced to become a sex slave.

Over the past twenty years, the sexual exploitation of children in Georgia has only become worse. Statistics show that

3,600 kids become victims of sex trafficking each year. That's enough children to fill 72 school buses.

My YA book is written with a dark, humorous bite, but child sex trafficking is a serious national problem. Anyone who needs help or wants to report possible human trafficking can call the National Human Trafficking Hotline at 1-877-373-8888.

ABOUT THE AUTHOR

Muriel Ellis Pritchett, born and raised in the city of Atlanta, graduated from the University of Georgia. The author of three fun fiction novels about feisty older women, Muriel was encouraged by her two daughters to write a YA paranormal thriller that they would enjoy reading. So she did. Muriel and her computer guru husband love traveling, good chocolate, computer games, *Star Wars*, and all things Disney.

NOTE FROM THE AUTHOR

Word-of-mouth is crucial for any author to succeed. If you enjoyed *Not Myself Today*, please leave a review online—anywhere you are able. Even if it's just a sentence or two. It would make all the difference and would be very much appreciated.

Thanks!
Muriel

Thank you so much for reading one of our
Young Adult Fiction novels.
If you enjoyed the experience, please check out our
recommended title for your next great read!

Dear Jane by Marina DelVecchio

"With sophisticated prose,
this gritty coming-of-age story blends
the familiar and the unthinkable
as the lead learns to use her voice."
-KIRKUS REVIEWS

View other Black Rose Writing titles at
www.blackrosewriting.com/books and use promo code
PRINT to receive a **20% discount** when purchasing.